"I'll walk you to your car..."

Eliana glanced back and an auburn tendril swept over her shoulder. "No, thanks. I'll meet you outside." Without waiting for his reply, she strode away.

Riker stepped back and looked at his dog. "What? The task force headquarters are little known to anyone. She'll be safe getting to her car."

The K-9 huffed his displeasure.

But once they exited the elevator, tiny hairs prickled his neck, and he spun. Sunlight beamed between the concrete pillars and diesel fumes stung his nostrils. No visual danger, but his senses said otherwise.

A revving engine roared from above, reverberating through the garage.

"Eliana!" Riker dropped his overnight duffel and bolted into a run, Ammo keeping in step with him.

A black sedan with tinted windows sped toward Eliana, who was strolling casually with her suitcase trailing behind her. Riker's hand flew to his hip and he withdrew his Glock, aiming for the car. "Eliana! Get down!"

She turned and her eyes widened at the quickly advancing sedan.

"Get down!"

But gunshots drowned out his words...

Sharee Stover is a Colorado native transplanted to Nebraska, where she lives with her husband, three children and two dogs. Her mother instilled in her a love of books before Sharee could read, along with the promise "if you can read, you can do anything." When she's not writing, she enjoys time with her family, long walks with her obnoxiously lovable German shepherd and crocheting. Find her at shareestover.com or on Twitter, @shareestover.

Books by Sharee Stover

Love Inspired Suspense

Secret Past
Silent Night Suspect
Untraceable Evidence
Grave Christmas Secrets
Cold Case Trail
Tracking Concealed Evidence
Framing the Marshal

Visit the Author Profile page at LoveInspired.com.

FRAMING THE MARSHAL

SHAREE STOVER

LOVE INSPIRED SUSPENSE

INSPIRATIONAL ROMANCE

Love Inspired® SUSPENSE

INSPIRATIONAL ROMANCE

ISBN-13: 978-1-335-58748-0

Framing the Marshal

Copyright © 2022 by Sharee Stover

For questions and comments about the quality of this book, please contact us at CustomerService@Harlequin.com.

Love Inspired
22 Adelaide St. West, 41st Floor
Toronto, Ontario M5H 4E3, Canada
www.LoveInspired.com

Printed in U.S.A.

He delivered me from my strong enemy, and from them which hated me: for they were too strong for me.
—*Psalm* 18:17

Special thanks to Heather Sargent
for taking time to discuss all things DNA with me.
Your brilliance made this story come to life.

ONE

Procrastination was the enemy, and it might kill US Marshal Riker Kastell if he didn't get home soon. Exhaustion tugged at his eyelids, compelling Riker into the battle for consciousness. If he surrendered, he'd fall asleep at the wheel of his pickup. "We should've left the cabin sooner. Let me guess, it's the turkey or deer's fault? You spotted it on your property and felt compelled to chase it away, then somehow got yourself stuck in the shed? I'm not blaming you. I'm just saying if you hadn't gone gallivanting off, forcing me to search for you—" A tongue swiped across his cheek, silencing the rebuke.

K-9 Ammo rested his head beside Riker's face, tail thumping against the back seat.

"You're forgiven, but remember, tomorrow while you're sleeping, I'll be doing neck aerobics in the morning briefing."

A whine of agreement or sympathy—Riker wasn't certain—conveyed Ammo's understanding.

He chuckled and took a sip of his coffee. "Not much longer. You owe me, dude, so keep me company. Not only did you break that slat in the shed, but you also had me searching all over Smith Falls for you."

His retired K-9 grunted and returned to his spot on the

back seat, out of Riker's reach. Within minutes, the dog's snoring filled the cab.

"Thanks for the backup." Riker flipped on the radio and cranked up the air conditioner.

After his team's successful takedown of several D'Alfo Nites's gang members, the Heartland Fugitive Task Force had earned a short vacation to recuperate and rejuvenate. Infused with fresh determination, Riker was eager to return to work. The only downside was the newest—and hopefully temporary—addition to the team, his ex high school girlfriend, Eliana Daines. The old wounds Eliana had inflicted on him nineteen years prior by abandoning him had planted a bitter root that had developed into a fully grown heart grudge. She'd left without a backward glance...until a month ago.

As though no time had passed between them, Eliana had contacted him and, in a professional manner, requested his help with PHACE, her new DNA phenotyping program. He'd wanted to refuse her, but Eliana still affected him more than he cared to admit. Another example of when procrastination supplemented by avoidance had reared its head and bit Riker. Instead of ignoring her completely, he'd politely referred her to his commander, assuming Beckham Walsh would do the ugly duty. To his dismay, Beckham and the team had welcomed Eliana's offer to beta test the revolutionary program. PHACE had played a significant role in the last takedown by successfully predicting the identification of several Nites. The program had compiled facial sketches, which resulted in the men's arrests for a series of home invasions, assaults and burglaries.

But dealing with Eliana was no effortless task. For all her beauty, she had the abrasiveness of a cactus and seemed oblivious to the wake she'd left behind in Riker's heart. She hadn't once tried to explain why she'd walked away from him. Additionally, her businesslike nature included her unrelenting comments regarding DNA's unbiased approach to investigations. She and Riker clashed at every interaction. If she said the word *biased* one more time, he might lose his cool.

PHACE had phenomenal capabilities, but Riker remained suspicious of any technology. He'd witnessed too many lazy investigators rely on the ease of a computer. Worse, he'd seen the effects of inaccurate results that ruined an innocent man's life. No innovative equipment replaced real cop work.

His ruminations provided the needed distraction to keep him awake for the rest of the drive home. When, at last, Riker pulled into his garage, fatigue hit with a vengeance and he prepared to surrender.

The overhead light failed to go on. Great, one more thing to fix in all his spare time.

He shut off the engine and twisted to look at his still sleeping dog, curled up in the back seat. "Wake up, dude. We're home."

His hard-of-hearing Dutch shepherd didn't move. Not unusual since the day they'd barely survived a grain elevator explosion that had stolen most of Ammo's keen auditory sense, resulting in his retirement from active duty.

Unable to reach his dog from the driver's seat, Riker would have to go around to the passenger side to wake him. Placing one boot on the concrete floor, he started to exit the vehicle when a force slammed his face into the steering wheel.

Pain blasted through his nose and his eyes watered, blurring his vision.

Stunned, Riker jerked upright.

Something encircled his throat from behind and tightened, preventing Riker from turning his head.

The assailant yanked him out of the truck then kicked the door shut.

Like a choke collar, his attacker pulled, straining the cord and cutting off Riker's oxygen supply. He stumbled back, complying with the unspoken demands to prevent his own strangulation while simultaneously fighting to regain his bearings.

With one hand, Riker tried to free himself, grasping wildly for the door with the other.

He staggered, gasping for air.

Desperate to break free, Riker's hands flew to his throat, searching for anything to escape the binding.

Stars danced in front of his eyes. He'd black out any second now.

Riker leaned forward, intending to fling the man over his back. His strength waned as the line cinched tighter, slowly cutting off his ability to breathe.

He swayed into the truck, catching a glimpse of his reflection in the window and the shadowed figure behind him.

Ammo barked and growled, clawing at the glass, desperate to get to his partner.

A strike to Riker's knees dropped him to the concrete floor.

Muffled woofing echoed in the distance.

Then a slam to the back of his head and everything went black.

From the depths of the darkness, distressed yelps dragged Riker conscious. His brain raged with a thousand piercing swords.

He groaned, forcing his eyes open, and blinked rapidly against the bright sunlight that sliced through the blinds across the wood floor.

Riker pushed himself to a sitting position and surveyed the familiar space of his living room. Confusion danced with the pain in his head. What happened?

Thoughts of the attack rushed at him, but he blanked after that. How did he get inside his house? Pressing the heel of his hand against his temple, Riker got to his feet, swaying, and staggered to the garage.

Ammo's barking grew louder.

He hurried through the hallway to the mudroom and slipped on the wet surface. Glancing down, he gasped.

A crimson pool formed beneath the man blocking the door.

Riker's thoughts raced as he scanned the face and unblinking eyes. The familiar D'Alfo Nites's snake neck tattoo confirmed his identity. Orion Potts, aka Moneyman, was dead in his mudroom.

How did Moneyman get into my house? Was he the one who attacked me last night?

Ammo's relentless whines diverted Riker's attention, and he carefully stepped over the body and walked into the garage. The outer door was closed, causing the dog's barks to echo in the space.

At his approach, the canine's pleas increased and he scratched furiously at the window.

"I'm coming. Hold on." Riker reached the pickup and released Ammo, who bounded out, greeting Riker in a flurry of tail-wagging and face-licking gratitude. "I missed you, too, buddy. Are you okay? Did he hurt you?" Kneeling unsteadily, he inspected Ammo for any injuries then exhaled relief at finding none.

Ammo offered a few last licks and whimpered in appreciation.

"Stay." Riker held up a palm, reiterating the command.

The Dutch shepherd dropped to a sit, quivering in obedience. Riker reached inside the truck and grabbed his phone, still sitting in the dashboard holder. His duty weapon remained in the console where he'd left it, no rounds missing. He withdrew Ammo's short leash and snapped it on the dog's collar.

"Okay, come on." They walked through the side door onto the lawn where Riker called Commander Beckham Walsh.

"I was about to send a rescue team to drag you into the office," Beckham said. "Vacation time is over."

"Moneyman is dead in my house." Riker launched into a speedy explanation of the events leading to his call.

"I'm on my way. Notify Omaha PD." Beckham disconnected.

"This is unreal," Riker mumbled.

After reporting the incident and being assured an Omaha officer was en route, Riker wandered his yard, searching for signs of forced entry.

Nothing.

Within a few minutes, a patrol unit pulled up in front of his Dundee District house. A short, portly man exited the vehicle and approached while casually withdrawing a notebook from his shirt pocket. "I'm Officer Marvin."

Riker extended a hand, which Marvin refused. "US deputy marshal Riker Kastell, and this is K-9 Ammo."

Marvin gave Riker and his canine companion a disinterested glance. "You reported an attack and a dead body?"

Riker retold the story, trailing the officer around the premises.

"You don't remember what happened?" Marvin quirked a skeptical eyebrow.

"No. The intruder knocked me out."

"Hmm." Disbelief oozed from the officer, and when they reached the garage, he halted. "The body is inside?"

"Yes, I'll show you—"

"No. Wait here." Marvin turned his back and entered the house.

Riker moved out to the lawn again. Several more Omaha

PD patrol cars pulled up and the responding officers passed, entering the side door of the garage without acknowledging him. Though he'd not expected such a cool reception, the behavior wasn't unusual considering the circumstances. Ammo remained beside him, and they meandered to the front porch and sat on the cement steps.

Beckham's black Suburban pulled up and parked behind Marvin's cruiser. A measure of relief comforted Riker until Eliana—impeccably dressed and attractive as ever—slid out of the passenger seat. He groaned and Ammo glanced up curiously. "What is *she* doing here?" he whispered, petting the dog.

As if hearing the conversation, Beckham closed the distance between them and explained. "Eliana and I were meeting when you called. Have paramedics examined you?" He scanned the area just as an ambulance arrived.

Riker shook his head, intensifying the pain in his skull and regretting his actions instantly. "No, but other than a raging headache, I'm fine."

"What happened?" Beckham asked.

Riker shot a glance at Eliana, but Beckham seemed oblivious to his silent plea to send the woman away. "I have no idea. Got home late from my cabin and someone attacked me. I literally have no memory of anything after that. I woke up on the living room floor then tripped over Moneyman in my mudroom." Riker gestured toward the door. "Officer Marvin and his teammates already have the we-don't-believe-you act going. Who am I kidding? I don't believe me."

Neighbors trickled out from their homes then loitered, curious, on their lawns.

"Let's take this inside," Beckham suggested.

They climbed the stairs to the house, but Marvin blocked the doorway. "Mr. Kastell, I must talk to you. Privately."

"This is my commander. Speak freely," Riker replied,

arms crossed over his chest. "It'll save me the time of repeating it to him later when my team arrives." Ammo remained close to his side.

Marvin stood taller and shot a frown at the K-9. "We're the investigating agency and cannot allow the scene to be contaminated."

"I'll stay out here with Ammo if you'd like," Eliana offered.

Riker glanced at Beckham, who responded with a slight nod. Reluctantly, Riker passed Eliana the leash, and she gently led him down the steps to the lawn.

"You're the lead, of course," Beckham answered in a politically diplomatic tone. "However, our task force brings a wealth of expertise, and the D'Alfo Nites are our top case right now. Combining efforts benefits everyone. Let's go inside."

Marvin huffed and spun on his heel, allowing them to enter the foyer only before halting. "This is as far as you will go until I've spoken with my captain. He will determine whether you're assisting in the investigation." Marvin spat the word *assisting*, as though it tasted bitter in his mouth. "For now, don't touch a thing. Our crime technician is collecting evidence." He gestured at a tall blonde near the hallway.

"HFTF's help is most appreciated, Officer," a baritone voice said from behind Riker.

"Captain Ferguson." Marvin blanched.

Riker turned.

Beckham stepped toward the newcomer. "Thanks for coming so quickly. This is Riker Kastell."

The captain extended a hand to Riker after shaking Beckham's. "Heartland Fugitive Task Force has a reputation of excellence. And I'm sure Officer Marvin is happy to *assist*."

Riker had to restrain his satisfied grin at Ferguson's emphasis on the last word.

"We were just getting the latest update," Beckham said.

Marvin's face burned so red, Riker thought the man would explode. "Captain Ferguson, with all due respect, this is a murder investigation and there is an obvious conflict of interest if HFTF investigates. Marshal Kastell was the only one with the deceased, Orion Potts."

"Don't say his name like he was some great guy. Moneyman was a fugitive wanted for multiple murders," Riker inserted.

"Moneyman?" Ferguson clarified. "D'Alfo Nites?"

"Yes, sir," Riker acknowledged.

"Regardless, there are no signs of forced entry, and Potts was shot at close range," Marvin concluded.

"I didn't invite him into my house to kill him," Riker said.

The evidence technician whispered to Marvin, passing him a clear plastic bag. "Thank you, Joy. This was found inside the deceased's denim pocket." Marvin handed the evidence bag to Riker.

He recognized the clipping of the familiar story the South Dakota newspaper had done before he'd joined the marshals. "Why would Moneyman have this old article and picture of my family?"

"You tell me," Marvin said.

"I'm sure I wouldn't know," Riker snapped, passing the bag to the tech.

The officer snorted. "We'll handle this investigation as per protocol. We don't give special favors regardless of the suspect's career."

"And you don't accuse without substantial evidence," Riker retorted.

"I think we all agree deputy marshal Kastell cannot investigate his own case, but it does not prohibit the rest of

our team from assisting," Beckham said. "We won't inter-
fere. However, we have fine resources, including a DNA
phenotyping program."

Riker opened his mouth to protest, but Ferguson spoke
first. "That is a welcomed offer. Joy, please work with Commander Walsh on the trace and DNA evidence you extract."

The crime scene tech nodded. "Absolutely."

Ferguson addressed Marvin. "Officer, I'd like to speak
with you." He ushered the clearly perturbed man away.

"I didn't kill Potts," Riker contended quietly.

"I believe you," Beckham assured him. "Trust the process."

"Riker," Eliana called from outside.

The men hurried down the steps, where Eliana pointed
to a black glove stuck under one of the rosebushes. "Look
what Ammo found."

Riker leaned closer, gaining a better view. "That's a mechanic's glove. I don't own any of those. What's it doing
here?"

"Maybe the killer dropped it on his way out." Beckham
called for the evidence tech, and she rushed out and quickly
documented the find.

"Always trust your dog." Riker patted Ammo with an
upward glance at Eliana. "Next to boots-on-the-ground
police work, they're the most reliable tool."

She visibly bristled. "True, but then dogs aren't biased."

Riker bit his tongue before offering a career-ending
comment. She shifted closer, permitting the coroner and a
paramedic to carry out the deceased.

"Please put a rush on that and submit a DNA sample to
my attention," Beckham instructed Joy.

"If you'd prefer to ride with me, you'll have the sample
immediately," she said.

"Actually, I only need the genetic code results," Eliana
interjected.

"Sure," Joy replied.

"A most generous offer, thank you." Beckham turned to Riker. "Leave your vehicle here and take my Suburban to the office. Plan for desk duty until this is resolved." He tossed Riker the keys.

"I'll clean up at the Rock." Riker referenced the team's headquarters, which also featured full shower and sleeping quarters. All members kept supplies and clothing there.

"The team will respond here, and we'll meet you when we have the evidence samples," Beckham said.

"Great, my fate lies in the hands of incompetent technology," Riker mumbled, rubbing his neck.

"We're in this fight with you, utilizing every available resource. Nobody gets away with attacking one of our own." Beckham turned to address Eliana. "Once PHACE develops the composite sketch, we'll have the face of our killer."

Eliana hovered over her laptop screen as PHACE completed the last eight percent of the facial composite sketch. The excruciating hours of waiting since she'd loaded the DNA code sample taken from the glove Ammo had found in the bushes had kept her on an emotional roller-coaster ride. Her stomach tightened with each tick of the conference room clock.

Two walls held state-of-the-art, sixty-inch monitors while windows comprised the others. From her seat at the expansive kidney-shaped table centered in the updated fourth-floor headquarters, she had a full view of the team's black desks, bordered by short cubicle walls and dog beds beside the respective handlers. The modern layout contrasted with the aged building's nondescript exterior, disguising their lair from the public. Commander Beckham Walsh's office door stood open at the far side. Immense windows peered out to Omaha's downtown Old Market and summer sunshine beamed in, providing ample light.

Eliana glanced up as Ammo accompanied Riker into the conference room, dubbed "the Rock" by the team. He passed her, wafting the fresh scent of soap. He'd combed his dark blond hair, still wet from his shower, and changed into a pair of black cargo pants and a tan shirt that spanned his muscled chest. Eliana's ears warmed, reminding her she'd appraised his appearance one second too long.

She averted her gaze and squeaked, "Hey."

Riker grunted a reply. True to his recent confrontational nature, he moved to the furthest possible seat at the table. Ammo paused by her as though he understood her anxiety.

"Hi, sweetie." She stroked his soft brindle fur. If only Riker was as welcoming as his K-9.

The palpable strain lingered, and she avoided glancing in Riker's direction, returning her attention to the computer. Animosity hovered around him in an invisible shield, making him unapproachable. She'd questioned her decision about contacting him at least a hundred times. And she always returned to the same conclusion. They'd met nineteen years ago for a reason. Riker's position with HFTF was no accident. His willingness to connect Eliana with the team proved he was the best resource. Thankfully, he'd not turned her away, but the emotional distance he maintained affirmed they were no longer friends. Regardless, Eliana pocketed her feelings for the sake of the end goal, even if it meant bearing Riker's obvious disdain.

Desperate to break the silence, she said, "Your team is like nothing I've ever seen before. Why do you call your headquarters the Rock?"

Riker leaned back in his chair. "The name reflects our strength in praying together and staying anchored to God in our missions."

Eliana smiled. "I love that." Every day she'd spent with

the task force had reinforced her desire to be a permanent part of the elite team, oozing integrity and cooperating with infectious synergy. PHACE might provide her that opportunity. "The system is at ninety-five percent completion."

From the corner of her eye, she glimpsed Riker's scowl, though she didn't miss the anticipation lingering in his expression too.

Eliana exhaled, willing herself to relax. PHACE had proved its value before and would do the same again. Her entire life rode on the success of the program. More importantly, the opportunity to reopen her brother's cold case lay in the hands of this elite team's endorsement. *Lord, You know my heart. I'm doing this for Hunter.*

Whatever it took, Eliana would ensure Hunter got the justice he deserved. Once she—and the task force—convinced Denver PD to utilize the DNA phenotyping program to process any physical evidence from his case to identify his killer.

At the time of Hunter's murder, the technology PHACE provided hadn't existed. Without the team's endorsement, Eliana couldn't run into Denver PD and demand they use her program. She was a nobody who'd devoted everything into developing the ultimate phenotyping program. All for solving Hunter's drive-by shooting. Because without PHACE, she was nothing more than the abused daughter of a con man criminal and the sister of a murder victim. Lest she have any doubts, she need only recall her deceased father's many cruel reminders.

First, she had to prove the system's value.

If the team knew her motives, they'd refuse to help her. She'd assisted them in the last case and won over Beckham Walsh.

Riker's investigation upped the stakes significantly.

Movement caught her attention as Beckham entered the office, trailed by one of the team members. Eliana searched her mind for the man's name. Grant? No, DEA agent Graham Kenyon. She gave herself a mental pat on the back for recalling his identity.

The men walked into the conference room.

"Ready?" Beckham flashed her a welcoming smile.

"Just about." Eliana stood and reached into her rolling suitcase for the cords needed to project her screen on the monitors. On second thought, maybe she should preview the results first. She opened her mouth as Beckham dropped into the chair beside her.

Or not.

"Let's see what your amazing program came up with."

"Should we wait for the rest of the team?" Eliana suggested.

"No, they're still working the scene," Beckham said.

So much for stalling.

Graham sat opposite Beckham, and Riker scooted to a closer seat. "Ammo, come."

The Dutch shepherd tilted his head in an almost apologetic glance before rising and sitting beside his partner.

"We're excited to see what PHACE produced," Graham said.

Me too. Eliana smiled and busied herself with the cords, certain they heard her heart pounding out of her chest. She finished the connection, hands shaking, and slid into the chair, wiping her palms on her dress slacks.

"So, if I remember from your last profiles—" Riker began.

"Composites." Eliana bit her lip, keeping her eyes on the screen. Why had she corrected him? As if he needed one more reason to dislike her.

Riker audibly sighed, clearly annoyed. "Same difference."

Nope, she couldn't ignore the incorrect information.

Eliana focused on him. "Actually, no. Think of DNA like

a recipe comprising each person's unique qualities. PHACE reads that recipe using DNA genotypes in combination with complex algorithms to develop a composite image. This allows us to predict the physical attributes of the person. By incorporating their eye and hair color, skin tone, facial shape and genetic ancestry, the system creates a color picture akin to a detailed police sketch." Talking about her program infused Eliana's excitement and confidence.

"Fascinating." Beckham nodded approval.

"PHACE stands for?" Graham asked.

Encouraged by the interest, Eliana said, "Phenotyping Hybrid Analytical Composite Effect."

"Nice," Graham replied.

"Joy provided a sample from the glove found at Riker's house," Eliana explained. "We confirmed Moneyman's blood on the outside, along with gunshot residue. Not surprising. Criminals often think they'll hide their identity by wearing gloves, but they don't understand they leave trace evidence inside. I ran that genetic code sample in PHACE."

Finally, the program opened and began drawing the composite sketch. Eliana held her breath, thankful the system was working. So far, it hadn't stopped or encountered any glitches. The cursor swept from left to right, like an artist painting the canvas.

Beckham's phone chimed and he glanced at the screen. "I need to take this."

Grateful for the interruption and a few minutes to finish the composite, Eliana nodded. The progress line read *ninety-nine percent complete*.

"Yes, thank you. Absolutely." Beckham disconnected and addressed them. "Captain Ferguson will accompany the team here once they've cleared the scene."

Riker groaned, hands behind his head. "Why are we letting Omaha PD handle the investigation?"

"We're cooperating with them," Graham corrected

with a grin. "Besides, we have the upper hand and a secret weapon with PHACE. It'll give us the face of our killer."

"Right, right," Riker mumbled. "Just remember, it's only a computer program. Not exact science. A prediction—as Eliana said—of what the person will look like."

Why did the man oppose her at every turn? "True, however, by compiling the composite sketch and running that against facial recognition software, we can ascertain with some certainty a suspect's identity," she replied coolly.

"Remember, Riker, this might solve the mystery killer question," Graham said.

Eliana shot him a smile of appreciation.

"Let's hope so, because I'm no murderer. If Officer Marvin has his way, they'll arrest me today," Riker grumbled, crossing his arms over his chest.

Eliana ignored him and pulled up the case file. Anticipation had her climbing out of her skin. *Please let this work, Lord.*

Her throat went dry.

The lower part of the face appeared, slowly moving upward to the forehead, until the form finished.

She gaped.

No.

The ticking of the clock coordinated with the blood drumming in her ears.

Eliana stiffened, her gaze bouncing between the men at the table. Her pulse quickened with nervousness. Three composite sketches lined up on the screen. Each depicted a man's face, but with slight variations for age, fashion, haircut and facial hairstyle. However, the similarity remained consistent. And unnerving.

They couldn't be correct. Or could they? Had she done something wrong? Eliana studied the formulas. Had she entered data incorrectly? She wasn't arrogant enough to think the program was infallible, but the result rattled her.

An image of Riker stared out at her from the computer screen.

Riker jumped to his feet. "Thank you for proving technology is useless. It's a picture of me." He stormed to the monitor closest to him and pointed at the screen. "You must've put in a sample from my house rather than the evidence. It's obviously incorrect."

"I was with Eliana when she entered the sample, Riker. I can attest to the accuracy and chain of custody," Beckham asserted.

"Maybe you have an evil twin," Graham said.

"Not all of us have identical siblings to blame things on," Riker shot back.

"Ouch." Graham winced. "I'm on your side. No need to attack."

"Sorry, bro, that was uncalled for," Riker replied. Then, facing Eliana, he barked, "You did something wrong."

She narrowed her eyes, choosing her next words carefully. "PHACE pulls from the evidence entered. If the glove is yours, it would explain a lot."

"And paints me a murderer," he challenged. "For the last time, I don't wear or buy mechanic's gloves. You made a mistake."

"PHACE produces unbiased results based on the DNA sample. There's no manipulation involved," Eliana blurted.

"Once again with the bias argument," Riker disputed. "Clearly it's wrong, because I didn't kill Potts, I don't wear mechanic's gloves, and I never shot my duty weapon."

"Which the ballistics evidence will confirm once it's finished," Beckham reassured him.

"What did the tox screen show?" Graham asked.

"You're hoping the killer drugged and forced me to shoot Moneyman?" Riker replied. "Negative on the drugs."

"Calm down, Riker. There's a logical explanation for this." Graham leaned forward to study the image.

Eliana scrolled on her computer, displaying rows of graphs, numbers and sequences. "The markers are all there and the profile is accurate. Agent Kenyon, your comment has me wondering. Familial DNA explains a physical resemblance. Riker, do you have siblings, cousins, anyone else who looks like you?"

Riker sighed. "My brother and I are ten years apart in age and not biologically related. I told you this was a waste of time. Time I don't have. We're back to square zero."

Beckham quirked a disapproving eyebrow, and Riker slid into his seat.

"We're still waiting on results from the other databases," Graham said.

"How about we do actual police work instead of depending on fallible technology? We've seen—" Riker gestured at the screen "—this is inaccurate. If the killer planted the glove, which I think he did, he used it to frame me for Potts's murder."

"Okay, how do we prove that?" Graham asked. At Riker's glare, he lifted his hands in surrender. "I'm working the clues. Let's talk it out."

Riker pushed away from the table again and paced in front of the monitor. "I don't know. They could've put it on my hand and shot Potts while I was unconscious. That explains the blood and trace DNA."

Eliana intertwined her fingers to reduce the nervous shaking. This was it. She'd messed up and lost every chance of winning the team's endorsement. *Not biologically related.* Riker's comment lingered. "Are you adopted?"

Riker exhaled like a parent speaking to an insolent child. "Yes."

"Do you know the details of your birth? You could have a sibling…a twin." The words tumbled out before she could stop them.

"I think my parents would've mentioned that important detail," Riker argued. "And we're not having a *This is Your Life* discussion right now. I didn't kill Potts. My word should be enough, but I know I'll need actual evidence to prove that. We don't have to show this composite to anyone. It's not fact or even an approved forensics database," Riker contended, and for the first time, Eliana saw fear in his eyes.

"Except Captain Ferguson is coming here to see the results. We will not hide or ignore the sketch," Beckham said. "Riker, rest assured the team will support you."

"We believe you're innocent," Graham agreed.

The men's words seemed to defuse Riker, and he slid into his chair. "Why are the Nites framing me? It's like they handpicked me, but our entire team worked on the last mission." He rested his head in his hands.

"For whatever reason, they've targeted you," Beckham said. "If we find out why, we'll have the key to the killer." His phone rang again. "It's the mayor's office."

Focused on Beckham, the group waited for information. His eyebrows furrowed and he rubbed his forehead as he listened and offered a simple, "Yes. Understood."

Eliana's pulse quickened.

He disconnected and told the group, "We have more problems." Beckham shook his head. "Word got out that Moneyman's body was found at Riker's home, as well as the successful results from PHACE in relation to our prior case involving the D'Alfo Nites's arrestees. They want to know if the program will be used in Riker's case. The mayor is demanding a press conference and interviews."

"Who leaked information in an ongoing investigation?" Riker's voice boomed.

"Great," Graham sighed. "Is the twin idea appealing now?"

The icy glare Riker shot his friend said he didn't appreciate the teasing.

Eliana contemplated the possibility of a familial relation. She sat straighter. "I'll talk with the media and explain how your team is focused on pursuing the arrest and apprehension of gangs in the area. If the Nites are framing Riker—"

"If?" Riker barked.

"—the positive exposure," Eliana continued, "will prove they have a motive behind the murder. A win for everyone, right?" Not to mention the publicity would help promote PHACE. A twinge of guilt at the selfish thought pricked at her conscience.

No one spoke for several long seconds, and her gaze bounced between the men.

What had she said wrong?

Riker leaned across the table. His normal expression of animosity had evaporated, replaced by concern. "Eliana, the press just handed you to the D'Alfo Nites by naming you responsible for identifying their posse. You made their kill list. They're coming for you too."

TWO

Riker studied Eliana while mentally berating himself for blurting out her endangered status with the delicacy of a hand grenade. In response to his harsh verbal reality check, her green eyes had widened to the size of dinner plates. She visibly swallowed and her skin blanched. Averting her gaze to her computer screen, she mumbled, "Oh."

Graham shook his head, conveying his disapproval, and Beckham's glare added to Riker's silent rebuke.

Ever the gentleman, Graham leaned forward, softening his voice. "What my colleague meant was, as a result of the ill-timed press release, the Nites will have reason to stop you from assisting in the investigation."

She glanced up, fear consuming her beautiful features.

Riker couldn't help but feel sorry for her. Danger and death threats were a normal part of his career, not hers. Ammo sidled up to Eliana, as though he understood exactly what she needed at that moment.

I'm here, ready to flip out, and you comfort Eliana. Traitor.

The sweet dog's presence seemed to calm her, and she visibly relaxed while stroking Ammo's head. Some days, the dog outsmarted him. Riker turned to Beckham. "Eliana needs protective custody."

"I agree," the commander said.

"I'm not leaving my house." She lifted her chin, defiance in her eyes.

He knew nothing about her life. Did she have an aging relative or child? Worse, did she have a boyfriend? The unbidden thought annoyed him. Why did he care? "It's not a request," Riker said.

"No," she repeated, shooting him a murderous glower. "Anyway, if what you said is true, won't the gang just follow me? Why would I risk anyone else's life? Can't you have an officer patrol my neighborhood?"

"I suppose that's understandable," Beckham said. "I'll arrange for an officer to provide protective coverage for you. However—" he flicked a glance at Riker "—Eliana isn't the only one in danger."

"I can take care of myself." Riker paused and surveyed his commander, who sat palming his cell phone.

Graham spoke first. "Boss, what aren't you saying?"

Beckham sighed and ran a hand over the back of his neck. "Because of the team's high profile, and the mounting circumstantial evidence, the mayor is pushing for formal charges. Specifically, Riker's arrest within seventy-two hours. Unless we can produce refuting evidence."

Riker slumped in his seat. "Is that all?" he groaned sarcastically.

"He's also aware Eliana is helping us," Beckham elaborated. "And he is interested in viewing the results PHACE produced in the prior D'Alfo Nites's case as well as what it creates in your case."

Riker jolted upright so fast, a zing of pain shot through his neck and back. "No!" He slammed both hands on the table, startling Eliana. "She's just a contractor, beta testing her program." He gestured widely toward the monitor, exasperated. If Beckham hadn't boasted about PHACE, they wouldn't have to factor it in the equation. No good would come from reminding his commander about that detail.

"And you said it yourself, all the evidence is circumstantial. My career speaks for itself. Surely, he sees I'm no criminal."

"The court of public opinion, or better, perception, speaks louder," Graham observed.

"Precisely," Beckham agreed.

"We don't have a second to waste and we can't set aside resources, including me. I need to help with the investigation. Even from the background." Riker leaned against the glass wall and crossed his arms to hide his shaking hands. He swallowed hard against Beckham's unwavering gaze. "Unless you think I'm guilty."

"That's not an issue. If I had any question about your integrity, you wouldn't be on this team," his commander assured him. "And as much as we value your brilliance, keeping this investigation aboveboard is our only viable option. I'm sorry, Riker, you can't be involved."

"He could provide protective detail for Eliana," Graham suggested, as if he was trying to help both Riker and Beckham.

Riker held up a hand. "No can do. I'm on admin leave, remember?"

"Desk duty," Beckham corrected. "Eliana, is there someone you can stay with?"

"Like I said, I don't want to leave my house. And I don't think assigning Riker to watch me is a good idea," Eliana argued.

He snapped a look at her. "Me either." A combination of relief and hurt at her dismissal left him confused with emotions he didn't have time to deal with.

"We've got your six," Graham interjected, using the slang that inferred their support.

Riker dropped his hands to his sides and exhaled. Whatever happened, his team's trust and belief in his innocence meant a lot. But their faith wouldn't withhold charges or keep him out of prison.

Beckham's phone rang again. "It's Captain Ferguson." He swiped the screen to answer.

Riker sucked in a breath, eavesdropping on every word.

"What?… And this person is credible? Willing to testify?" Beckham scribbled on a notepad. "What time did they see this?… Okay. Thanks." He disconnected and looked at Riker. "One of your neighbors said they witnessed you, or someone matching your description, walking into the house with Moneyman shortly after midnight."

"That's ridiculous!" Riker bellowed. "I was driving home. It wasn't me!"

"Let's hope your GPS tracker was working. That'll help." Beckham leaned back in his chair. "We have to show solid evidence and an unprejudiced investigation."

"I'm no cold-blooded killer," Riker repeated, sounding like a broken record. "Whoever is out to frame me won't stop until I'm convicted. Find who leaked the information to the press. Start with Officer Marvin. I'm suspicious of his confrontational attitude and determination to keep me from the case. Not to mention, he was the first on scene. Maybe he's in on it."

Beckham held up a hand. "Now hold on. We're not accusing anyone. Let's work this case with the care and quality we normally would." Riker opened his mouth to protest and Beckham continued. "I understand you're upset. I am, too, but the fact remains, word is out, and we can't unring a bell. Graham, get to Riker's house and update the team. We need to run interference before the press descends like vultures on roadkill."

"Roger that." Graham bolted from the room.

"Riker, stay off the grid and keep in touch with me. Most of all, be safe." Beckham's authoritative tone left nothing up for discussion. "The evidence we found was no accident. Whoever is out to frame you has taken significant effort to make sure you go down for Moneyman's murder. As it stands right now, there's not a lot in your favor."

Riker swallowed the rock lodged in his throat at the not-needed reminder.

"Sir, how can I help?" Eliana interjected.

Riker did a double take. "You and your program have done enough." Surely, Beckham wouldn't allow her to participate.

She narrowed her emerald eyes. "PHACE creates composites based upon what's fed into it. I'm certain there's a logical explanation for the composite's prediction of the killer's appearance."

"Are you saying PHACE is inaccurate?" Riker challenged. "Isn't it unbiased?"

"Eliana…" Beckham hesitated then said, "Is it possible a Riker look-alike explains the witness's account and the composite?"

She tilted her head. "It's possible. But DNA evidence doesn't lie, even though it can be placed at a crime scene to frame someone. I'll stay here and dig through the coding and DNA markers."

Beckham cleared his throat. "Unfortunately, that's not an option."

Wait. For the first time, there was a plausible solution to Eliana's stupid program and Beckham was denying her the opportunity to help Riker?

"Boss—" he objected.

As though Riker hadn't spoken, Beckham said, "The team will use the conference room and office to discuss confidential findings. As an outside contractor, you're not privy to the other details of the investigation."

"Of course." Eliana's cheeks bloomed into a becoming rose hue, and she glanced down. "I apologize for my assumption."

"No apologies." Beckham added, "Your assistance in

working on the composite is essential. It just cannot happen here."

Riker exhaled, silently contemplating whether Eliana was aiding his case or making it worse. He struggled to read her expressions, but Beckham's response indicated he wouldn't dismiss PHACE's results.

"May I work from home?" Eliana countered. "I want to start at the beginning. Perhaps run a second sample."

"Great idea, as long as chain-of-custody protocols are followed." Beckham folded his portfolio closed. "I'll order protective detail for you there."

Eliana pursed her lips. "That's unnecessary—"

"It's not an option." Beckham waved his hand dismissively. "We'll have enough issues defending why we're not releasing the composite immediately. I'll delay the mayor for the seventy-two hours, but I'm doubtful he'll wait much longer. If the public perceives we've tainted the investigation, Omaha PD will hijack the investigation and release us."

"Understood." Eliana closed the laptop. "I'll update you with my progress and findings."

"Thank you," Beckham replied.

Riker stood mute as they discussed his future, desperation building. "If she's working on my case, why can't I?" The blurted response made him sound like a childish brat. Eager to regain his confidence, he added, "I'll stay out of the limelight, but let me help behind the scenes."

"Negative. It's a complete conflict of interest."

"It's all in my interest and this is my team too. The D'Alfo Nites mission is my mission," Riker argued, anger returning.

"Go to your cabin." Beckham's voice held a warning. "We'll keep you apprised of any developments."

"My cell reception is sparse out there." Beckham's unwavering stance had Riker conceding. "Fine. I'll establish regular check-in times with you. What other options do I have since my house is an active crime scene? Ammo and I will work on the cabin."

At the mention of his name, his K-9 ears perked and he tilted his head. A twinge of hope soared in Riker's heart. Perhaps the veterinarian was wrong and the dog's hearing had returned?

Turning his back slightly, Riker tested the possibility using a familiar term that normally infused Ammo with energy and excitement. "I'll need to pick up new bacon treats on the way out of town."

Beckham's frown conveyed his understanding of Riker's attempt, but a gentle shake of his head dwindled Riker's hope. Ammo got to his feet, stretching and yawning—oblivious to the bacon offer. Disappointment returned.

The chime of Beckham's phone interrupted them again. "I need to take this. Riker, accompany Eliana home and wait until the officer arrives."

"Roger that."

"Keep the faith." Phone pressed against his ear, Beckham exited the conference room and walked to his office, closing the door behind him.

If not for the support of his commander and team, hopelessness threatened to consume Riker.

"I appreciate your offer to follow me home but, really, I'll be fine until the officer arrives." Eliana collected her laptop and cords.

"I didn't offer. I have direct orders," Riker remarked coolly.

She rolled her eyes and sighed. "Either way, it's unnecessary."

Did her brushoff indicate her disbelief in his innocence? "I suppose you think the team has a biased approach because they're not handing over your composite."

She blinked, pausing in place. "What? No."

"It's okay. I don't expect you to—"

"Riker!"

He clamped his mouth shut and Eliana persisted. "It's been a long time since we've talked—"

"I'm not the one who took off without a word."

Eliana slid into the chair; shoulders slumped. "No. That's on me."

The tension in his neck lightened but he stood frozen by her admission.

"The man I knew nineteen years ago was no cold-blooded killer." Eliana met his gaze, her green eyes probing his heart. "I've spent my life building PHACE. To say I don't believe in the program is hypocritical. However, I'm not contending the composite is inaccurate."

"You can't have it both ways." He pushed the chair under the table, creating distance to maintain his defensive armor.

"I trust in the infallible root of science—in this case, computer science—and because PHACE has no opinion on this matter—"

"No bias," Riker inserted.

She nodded. "I want to understand why it developed the composite."

"But that means your program is wrong."

"Or that I need to incorporate additional factors. Like familial connections." She resumed gathering her possessions.

"You believe I'm innocent?"

"Of murder? Yes." She shot him the unmistakable side grin that weakened his knees, and he quickly averted his gaze.

Ammo strode to the door, tail wagging. "Give me a few minutes to pick up some things from my desk before we go," he said, desperate to escape the conference room. "Stay." He reinforced the command by lifting a hand. The dog obediently sat beside Eliana, allowing Riker to slip out.

From the corner of his eye, he spotted her stroking Ammo's head and scruff. Though he couldn't hear her words, based on his dog's expression of adoration, the K-9 soaked up the attention.

I know, buddy, she's hard to refuse.

Riker shook off the thought and moved to his desk where his collection of law enforcement patches covered the partition wall. Fingering the US Marshal patch, he surveyed the others and sighed. *Please, God, help me.* He'd offer a lengthy prayer, but relying on the cry of his heart to express his fears was authentic. A horrible lie would steal the career he'd built and destroy his dreams. He surveyed the surrounding workspaces, envisioning his teammates in their chairs. The past years working with them had bonded them, and they functioned more like family than co-workers, unified in their faith and the mission of capturing dangerous fugitives.

He glanced at a daily update document on his desk, which detailed recent crimes courtesy of the Nites, who swept heinous acts of violence, drugs and human trafficking across the country faster than a tornado on the Nebraska plains. Though the task force had apprehended several members, it seemed for every criminal they arrested, three more emerged, like rats after the lights went out. And now the team's efforts, which should be focused on the Nites, would be wasted fighting for Riker.

And yet he depended on them to fight for him.

He gathered his laptop and charger, placing them in the overnight duffel he stored in his desk. Then he collected the keys from the lockbox for the unmarked loaner truck. Returning to the conference room, he spotted Eliana slipping her computer into a small rolling suitcase.

Ammo remained beside her. At his approach, the dog rose and walked to him, tail wagging. He nudged Riker's hand with his nose. "Hey, buddy, ready to go?"

Ammo gave an approving woof as Riker snapped on his leather leash.

Eliana stood. "All set."

They exited the headquarters and Riker prayed it wouldn't be the last time he'd serve in the office. He depressed the elevator button. "I'll have to follow your vehicle."

"I'm in the visitor lot." Eliana referred to community parking located on the corner the building shared with several surrounding offices.

Riker held open the steel doors and Eliana entered first. She'd already pushed their respective level buttons.

"I'll meet you on Farnam Street. We park the loaner vehicles in the garage."

"I'm in the orange SUV," she said.

Faint music played in the elevator, and Eliana's signature perfume filled the space. Her gray dress pants swayed gracefully over the tops of her simple black pumps and a chunky flower necklace accentuated the pale pink blouse she wore. She oozed class.

Riker averted his eyes, catching sight of Ammo, who shot him a get-a-grip-dude look. At the main level, Eliana stepped out, dragging her suitcase behind her.

Riker extended a hand, halting the doors. "Wait. I'll walk you to your car."

She glanced back, sweeping an auburn tendril over her shoulder. "No, thanks. I'll meet you outside." Without waiting for his reply, she strode away.

Reluctantly, Riker stepped back and was just about to change his mind and go after her, whether she wanted his protection or not, when the elevator door closed and proceeded to the underground level. Ammo tilted his head. "What? The task force headquarters is little known to anyone. She'll be safe getting to her car."

The K-9 huffed his displeasure.

Once they exited the elevator, Riker aimed for the far side where the team's white F-150 sat. Tiny hairs prickled his neck and he spun. Sunlight beamed between the concrete pillars and diesel fumes stung his nostrils. No visual danger, but his senses said otherwise.

He glanced at the ramp to the upper level, unable to shake the unsettling feeling that crept between his shoulder blades.

A revving engine roared from above, reverberating through the garage.

"Eliana!" Riker dropped his overnight duffel and bolted into a run, Ammo keeping in step with him.

They rounded a concrete pillar and sprinted up the ramp. A black sedan with tinted windows sped toward Eliana, strolling casually with her suitcase trailing behind her. Riker's hand flew to his hip and he withdrew his Glock, aiming for the car. "Eliana! Get down!"

She turned and her eyes widened at the quickly advancing sedan.

"Get down!" Gunshots drowned out Riker's repeated order.

Rapid fire consumed the atmosphere, and Eliana dove for shelter behind the closest object, a parked Jaguar. She scurried to sit and yanked her rolling suitcase close, hugging the bag for comfort.

Bullets shattered the windows, raining glass on her and melding with the weapon's rhythmic rat-a-tat-tat. Eliana tucked her face onto her knees, wrapping her arms over her head. Then, as fast as it began, the shooters sped away, screeching tires fading around the block.

Eliana crawled over the fragments of glass to peer around the quarter panel. Riker and Ammo rushed toward her, and she pushed to a standing position, exhaling relief.

"Are you ok—" A revving engine roared closer, cutting off Riker's question.

They took cover behind the bullet-pierced Jaguar as a repeat rendition of bullets blasted around them.

Eliana ducked her face in Ammo's neck, thankful he'd moved protectively in front of her. Riker returned fire and tires squealed as the second car sped away.

Her heart drummed in her rib cage. "Think they're gone?"

"Yeah." Riker dropped to a squat, pulling her into his arms. "Are you okay?"

Though her mind refused the comforting gesture, adrenaline shook her body and she succumbed to his touch. Eliana fought to breathe past the tightening of her chest.

"I'm here." Riker's breath was warm against her cheek.

She welcomed the embrace, absorbing his strength while processing the horrific events. *Get a hold of yourself.* Tears threatened. No. She would not show weakness. Eliana blinked them away. Placing her hands on Riker's broad shoulders, she pushed back and got to her feet. "Thanks. I'm fine now."

She refused to look at him, knowing if she saw kindness or compassion in his blue irises, she'd fall apart. Instead, she focused on her gray dress slacks, ripped from her dive into the pavement. Minor scrapes and cuts appeared on her palms, and she wiped them against the ruined garment.

Riker smoothed Ammo's brindle fur. "Good job, dude."

"They didn't hurt him, did they?"

"Nope, but let's move away from the glass so he doesn't cut his paws."

Eliana mutely complied and turned to face the lot located on the street corner. Gathering her rolling suitcase handle, she shuffled forward, and Riker strode beside her. The damage to her orange SUV became more apparent as she quickened her pace, closing the distance. Aghast, she slowed and inspected her vehicle. The shooters had blown out every window, and small holes pierced the metal in a strange case of bulleted chicken pox. A gasp escaped her lips.

She stumbled into Riker. "I'm so sorry." He extended a hand to her, but Eliana stepped out of reach, refusing to turn and look at him. The tears welling in her eyes became harder to repress.

"Is there anything you need to get out of it right now?"

"No," she whispered.

Numbly, she meandered toward the passenger side. *It's just a vehicle.* Except it was also her only mode of transportation. How would she afford to fix the damage? Was it beyond repair?

Riker reported the incident to a 9-1-1 dispatcher, giving Eliana a few minutes of solitude. Her gaze traveled down the side of the SUV to her rolling suitcase, surprised she still gripped the handle. She exhaled a silent prayer of gratitude. The bag containing her laptop remained unharmed. That was a big win.

"Cops are en route, and Commander Walsh is on his way down to deal with the report," Riker said, invading her thoughts.

She nodded, reaching into her purse to withdraw her key fob. She pressed the unlock button and the responding click jolted her into reality. The ludicrous action had her bursting into giggles. Not a window remained, gaping holes consumed the body, and she unlocked the door? The tears she'd held back streamed down her face.

"Eliana?"

She stifled the badly timed laughter and swiped away the moisture on her cheeks. Unable to speak through her giggles, she turned and showed the key fob to Riker. He grinned. "Probably don't need that now."

"Right?" Still chuckling, she tucked the key back into her purse.

Riker and Ammo watched her with curiosity and confusion written in their expressions. "I'm sorry you're caught up in this tangled web."

"It's not your fault," Eliana said, sincerity in the words. "Thank you for coming to my rescue."

"I'm just glad you responded as fast as you did. Ducking behind that car was smart."

She lifted a shoulder in a dismissive shrug. "Do you think they were targeting me or was it random?"

"Sadly, drive-by shootings are a little too common thanks to the Nites sweeping through Omaha with the force of a plague. But today's incident wasn't coincidence."

"They meant to kill me." Eliana surveyed the area. Most of the cars parked in the lot had sustained some damage. "They certainly attacked with a broad brush."

"This is an example of why we have to get the criminals behind bars. You're in danger until we do." He winced. "Sorry, the team is always harping on me about my delivery technique. I have a way of blurting the truth in a not-very-compassionate way. I just don't want anything to happen to you."

The vulnerability in his eyes chipped at her defenses. "I appreciate your candidness." She pressed a hand against his upper arm, surprised by the solid muscle. Warmth radiated up her cheeks, betraying her emotions, and she quickly withdrew from him. "You're not safe until they find the killer. That puts us in the same predicament."

"Can't argue against that."

Siren screams drew closer.

"We'd better get moving," Eliana suggested, lifting her rolling bag's handle.

They crossed the parking lot and headed for the underground garage, where Beckham stood shadowed beneath the building's ceiling. "Are you both okay?"

"A little shook up but alive," Riker said, providing an exceptional summary of the events leading up to and following the shooting.

"I had a great view from my office of the entire thing," Beckham said. "They could've killed an innocent bystander."

Eliana looked down, the words hitting her in the face like a cold glass of water. She couldn't agree more. Innocent people died in drive-by shootings too often. She should know. That's how she'd lost her brother, Hunter. All the more reason to ensure the task force endorsed PHACE.

"Eliana, I'll handle your vehicle's towing," Beckham said, regaining her attention. "Is there anything else I can do to help you?"

Yes, please give me a full-time position with the task force so I can pay for repairs. "No, sir, but thank you," she replied. "Thanks to Riker's quick response, we survived to battle another day with the Nites."

He shot her what she surmised was an appreciative grin, revealing the dimples in his cheek before glancing at Ammo.

"Are you certain they weren't targeting you in the drive-by shooting, Riker?" Beckham asked.

"Sir, I was in the parking garage when it began," Riker replied. "No doubt the Nites will try to keep Eliana from testifying to PHACE's contribution in the last sting."

Beckham sighed, surveying the area. "Yeah, you're right."

"This is proof she's on their kill list." Riker winced again and mouthed, *Sorry*, before continuing. "It's no coincidence the drive-by shooting happened when it did."

"Then you're both sporting targets on your backs," Beckham said.

"Agreed, and the Nites are persistent. They won't stop, no matter what it takes," Riker related. "As much as I like my freedom, sir, it's not about the seventy-two hours anymore. Finding Moneyman's killer is about our survival."

Eliana clenched her jaw, regretting that she'd encouraged Riker's candidness. Cloud cover darkened the sky and a breeze fluttered her hair. But the discussion and his last comment sent an icy shiver down her spine that had nothing to do with the weather conditions.

Riker lifted Ammo's leash. "We're headed to Eliana's place in Fremont now."

As the men discussed details, Eliana studied Riker. At an estimated six-foot-four, his broad shoulders and black combat boots made him appear taller. He practically oozed masculinity in everything he did and the way he handled himself. He'd grown up a lot since high school, but Eliana still saw the younger Riker behind his mature chiseled features.

"Be careful and watch for tails," Beckham said, jerking her to the current reality. "I'll make sure an officer is waiting for you."

"Roger that," Riker said.

The sirens grew closer. "Get out of here. I'll handle the report," Beckham said.

"We'll be in touch." Riker placed a palm against the small of her back and guided her deeper into the garage.

Eliana lifted her hand in a slight wave and strode with Riker through the empty space. Her favorite black pumps—scraped beyond repair, thanks to the drive-by fiasco—clicked in a staccato rhythm on the cement. Riker gathered his duffel bag lying on the floor.

When they reached a white F-150, he opened the rear doors, placing Eliana's rolling suitcase on the floorboard as she settled into the passenger seat. She flipped down the visor mirror, cringing at her wildly out-of-place auburn strands, and quickly fingered through the knots before straightening her blouse. A hole in the pale pink silk and the destruction to her slacks testified both were goners.

Riker loaded Ammo and then slid in behind the wheel. He seemed to survey her for several long minutes.

"I didn't dress for a danger dash through the Old Market," she quipped, brushing off her pants though no dirt lingered there.

"You still look great."

Surprised by the compliment, she looked up, but Riker started the engine and averted his gaze to the windshield. Within seconds, they rumbled out, using an alternative garage exit, avoiding the police presence on the opposite street.

They remained silent until Riker merged onto the highway, leaving Omaha city limits. His cell rang and he answered using his hands-free Bluetooth device.

"Report is done, and Eliana's SUV is en route to Cody's Body Repair," Beckham advised.

"Thank you," Eliana replied.

"Sir, I'm sure whomever is assigned to Eliana's protective detail will do a good job. But they should be aware that the Nites are relentless. They'll blindside an unprepared small-town cop—"

"Riker, discussion closed. It's handled." The finality with which the commander responded to Riker's question said he'd made up his mind.

Regardless, if she'd had any doubt before the drive-by shooting, their conversation confirmed what Eliana dreaded.

Someone wanted her dead.

THREE

It's handled. Commander Beckham Walsh's not-so-subtle expression of *leave it alone* grated Riker's cheese. Pride might be obstructing his reasoning, but he couldn't stop obsessing about his boss's underlying meaning. Was Beckham implying he didn't trust Riker? Even though he'd claimed to believe in Riker's innocence, were these words an unspoken inference about his doubts? Or did he blame Riker for Eliana's near-death experience outside headquarters? Whatever the reason, real or imagined, the bottom line remained the same.

Riker had to find Moneyman's killer, and Eliana needed competent protection. The sooner he handed her over to the care of an officer, the sooner he'd get busy working his case.

"Turn here." Eliana's voice jerked him out of his contemplations.

Riker yanked the wheel, narrowly missing the merge off Highway 275 into Fremont. "Sorry about that. My brain is all over the place."

"It's been quite a day." Eliana leaned back in the seat. "I'm glad to be out of Omaha, though. I seriously doubt a gang member will drive all this way to hurt me."

Except geography was no obstacle for the Nites. They spanned the country with members both identified and covert. He glanced at Eliana, loath to disturb her softened features and the false sense of peace with the truth. It was his job to worry about her so that she didn't live in fear. She might appreciate his candor, but she didn't need to hear it over and over. Riker clamped his jaw shut to refrain from speaking.

"Once we get through the night without incident, it'll prove I don't need protective detail."

He struggled to maintain a noncommittal expression.

"No offense," she quickly added.

"None taken. However, that'll be between you and Commander Walsh. I'm not into disregarding his orders." He gave her a sideways grin. "You've never seen the man angry."

They entered a residential area and he slowed, surveying the neighborhood. Mature elm trees bordered the older, well-maintained homes in perfect rows on either side of the street. Referring to the place as quaint made him sound too much like his mother, but the term adequately described the scene.

Though a hundred topics besides Beckham's approval entered his mind, the biggest one Riker refused to ask about—namely, his and Eliana's past—remained unspoken. They both had more than enough to contend with and discussing ancient history changed none of it.

Instead, Riker had spent the forty-five-minute commute silently developing his plan to secretly contribute to his investigation. The only hindrance was the unfamiliar protective anxiety he felt for Eliana's safety. Once he'd assessed the protective officer's level of preparedness, he'd feel better about leaving her.

"It's the little blue one on the right." Eliana gestured toward a squatty clapboard house.

A Fremont PD cruiser sat in front of the home. *Okay. Here we go.* Riker parked in the driveway and left the engine running. He turned to Eliana. "Stay here with Ammo while I talk with the officer and clear the house."

"The back door is always unlocked."

He did a double take. "That changes now, starting with this truck as soon as I step out. No unlocked doors."

She smiled sweetly. "Will do."

Riker exited the vehicle and strode to the patrol car, surprised when the officer rolled down the window. The gesture, though friendly, showed the guy wasn't protection-duty-detail material. Proper protocol called for an offensive approach. What if Riker had been a Nite?

The driver's door swung open and Riker instinctively reached for his weapon.

"Well, ain't this something?"

Riker instantly recognized the baritone rumble before his friend unfolded all six feet six inches, two hundred fifty pounds of himself from the police cruiser. "Nelson Van-Muse, is that really you?"

In one stride, Nelson met him. "Bro, like they made two such fine specimens? Please, I'm an original." With a hearty guffaw, he snagged Riker's hand, pumping his arm with gusto and a wide grin.

"Good to see you." Riker glanced at the house. "Gimme a second." He withdrew his Glock. "I need to clear the residence."

"I've got your six." Nelson reached for his duty weapon.

"Thanks." Rounding the front of the cruiser, Riker hurried toward the house, scanning the area for any unforeseen dangers. With an affirmative glance over his shoulder to Nelson, Riker entered through the unlocked back door.

Cinnamon and cloves assailed his senses as he maneuvered expertly through the single-floor home. Eliana's taste included white Victorian lace on just about everything from curtains to bedspreads, while varying shades of pink paint covered every wall. His mom would love her.

Three bedrooms—the smallest of which she'd converted into an office—a compact kitchen and dining room combination, one bathroom, and a medium-sized living room comprised the spotless home.

Riker exited the house through the back door and crossed the yard, admiring the mature maple trees that bordered the far side. He peered between the massive trunks where a creek ran parallel to Eliana's property. The high-water level was too wide to cross without the assistance of a bridge or plank to the opposite side where tall cornstalks, thick with leaves, consumed the land in a sea of green. Satisfied the area was safe, he strode through the well-manicured grass and rounded the house, while holstering his weapon.

Nelson remained on guard and visibly relaxed at Riker's return. "All clear."

"Alrighty."

Awareness hit Riker at his friend's mischievous grin. "You already did it before I got here."

"Maybe." Nelson shrugged. "You probably did a better job."

Riker laughed and slapped his friend on the back. "So good to see you! How long has it been?"

"Long enough that you think I've forgotten it's your turn to pay for the fries." Nelson chuckled.

"Right." Riker grinned. "When all this is over, let's definitely catch up over a couple of burgers."

Nelson led the way, and Riker studied the cruiser. "I thought you were with Lincoln PD?"

"Once we found out baby number seven was joining our crew, my beautiful bride insisted we return to Fremont to be closer to her family."

"Still hoping for a boy?" Riker teased.

Nelson chortled. "Healthy is my only request."

"Fair enough."

"You still married to the job?"

Unbidden thoughts of Eliana intruded Riker's mind. "Always."

Nelson's expression sobered. "Hey, man, is it true? What the news is saying about the murder?"

"Depends on what you've heard." Riker looked down. "Moneyman is dead, but it's an ongoing investigation—"

Nelson held up a hand, indicating he understood the necessity for confidentiality. "God knows what you need. I'm praying for you."

The promise touched Riker, lodging an emotional log in his throat. "You know I'd tell you the gruesome facts if I could."

"Your team are the superheroes of the law enforcement world. You'll have this wrapped up in no time. Then you can give me all the juicy specifics." Nelson added, "Over fries."

Riker grinned. "Count on it. Hey, I noticed the creek behind the house is running high."

"Yeah, saw that too. Extra line of defense since nobody will cross that, at least not without a bridge or help. And first they'd have to wade through that ocean of corn."

Riker mulled over the words. Should he offer to stay and assist? No. He needed to find Moneyman's killer. He glanced at the truck, where Eliana watched him curiously.

Nelson put a beefy hand on his shoulder. "I got this."

"You're right." Nelson's military career spoke for itself. Riker had no intention of insulting his friend by implying he was inept. "I feel better leaving Eliana—er, Miss Daines—in your capable hands."

"Commander Walsh didn't tell me who I was protecting. For real? Eliana Daines?" He peered past Riker and lowered his voice. "As in your first love, who you never talk about?"

"One and the same. And I'm still not talking about her." Riker grinned.

"A man's got a right to his secrets."

Of all the cops Beckham could've assigned, Nelson Van-Muse wasn't one Riker would have assumed would handle Eliana's detail. In all fairness, he'd not known his friend had changed departments. Riker trusted Nelson implicitly. "I understand it's not protocol, but would you keep me updated on the status here?"

Nelson nodded. "Absolutely."

"Thanks." Riker strode to the pickup and gestured for Eliana to unlock the doors. He leaned into the driver's side and killed the engine. "All clear. Let me introduce you to the officer providing your protective detail."

"I assumed by the way you chatted that you knew him." Eliana pushed open her door.

"Yes, he's an old friend." Riker leashed Ammo and he hopped down from the truck.

The trio approached Nelson's cruiser, and after a thorough boot sniffing, Ammo gave his double-time, tail-wagging approval.

"Hey, pup." Nelson held out a hand, allowing the dog to sniff first before stroking his head. "You're looking handsome as ever."

Riker gestured for Ammo to sit and he dropped to his haunches at Nelson's feet. "Eliana Daines, this is one of Nebraska's very best, Officer Nelson VanMuse."

His friend enveloped Eliana's hand in a firm shake. "Pleased to meet you, ma'am."

"Thank you for doing this," she said. "I'm sure you've got bigger and better things to deal with than wasting time watching my house."

"Are you kidding? I live for this stuff." Nelson passed her a business card. "My cell number is on there. Text or call if you need anything at all. No matter what time it is."

"I appreciate that."

"We should get you inside," Riker said.

Nelson slapped him a little harder than necessary on the

back before opening his car door and announcing, "I'd better return to my mobile office."

Eliana led the way to the front steps and turned, pausing. He took the unspoken cue as a hint that their journey ended there. For the second time since arriving at her home, he squelched disappointment. Offering his own business card, Riker said, "My personal cell is on here. If you need anything, don't hesitate to call."

Her fingertips brushed his hand as she accepted the proffered card. "I'll text you both, so you'll have my number too."

"Good." Riker searched his mind for an excuse to linger. Why? He needed to get busy. Eliana's safety came first, and keeping her outside was selfish and unwise. "Guess Ammo and I will get a move on. Ready, dude?"

His dog trotted to the full extent of his twenty-foot leash, actively sniffing a path around the lawn.

"He's either ignoring you, or he didn't hear you," Eliana said.

"Most likely both."

"He's not old and his muzzle isn't graying." She blinked and seemed to study Ammo. "Aren't dogs equipped with super auditory abilities?"

"Ammo was at the top of his game until a D'Alfo Nite set an explosion in a grain elevator that nearly killed us. We healed from the outer wounds, but the attack stole much of his hearing. Doc says it's possible he'll recover, so I'm reasonably optimistic."

"Oh," Eliana gasped. "I'm so sorry."

"He's unofficially retired. Though his physical capabilities aren't in question, a K-9 with compromised auditory skills can't qualify to work. Whenever possible, I take him with me. He gets depressed if he's left at home alone for too long."

"Dogs get depressed?" Eliana tilted her head, unbelieving.

"Absolutely. Especially working K-9s. They live for the job, and if that's taken away, it destroys a part of them. He's multicertified in tracking, apprehension, and explosion detection. Provided he's leashed, relatively close enough to hear and/or see me and can follow visual commands, the team uses him. Unofficially."

"Poor guy."

Shifting discussion gears, he jerked a chin toward Nelson's unit. "I know it's weird to have him outside but, please, don't discount anything. If something feels wrong, or if you're scared, contact Nelson. He is truly one of the best. He'll take good care of you."

A strange urge to stay confused Riker and, once more, he regretted not being assigned to do her detail.

"So, you're headed to your cabin?" She shifted from one foot to another then leaned against the iron porch railing. "Located where?"

"Smith Falls near Valentine." He swallowed, averting his gaze with the realization he'd be four hours away from her. "After our last visit, Ammo took off and, after two hours of searching, I found him stuck in the toolshed behind my cabin. He'd nudged through a broken slat. Can't be upset with him, though. If he doesn't see or hear me, he won't obey."

She turned to look at Ammo. "He must've found something interesting."

Riker chuckled. "Probably." He tugged on the leash and waved at Nelson. "We'd better get going."

"Thanks again for saving my life today."

"All in a day's work," he quipped. They remained there for several long seconds and Riker rocked back on his heels. *Awkward.* "Why not text Nelson and myself so we have your phone number?"

"Right. Good idea." Eliana withdrew her phone and

Riker recited his and Nelson's numbers. "Okay. I just sent one message with all three of us in it."

A second later, his cell chimed with a group text notification, and Nelson responded with a thumbs up emoticon.

With no other reasons to linger, Riker said, "Alrighty, I'll see you later."

He walked down the porch steps and straight to the pickup before he did anything stupid, like pull Eliana into his arms and promise to never let her go again. What was wrong with him?

Riker loaded Ammo into the pickup and slid behind the wheel. With one last wave, he shifted into Reverse and backed out of the driveway. As he approached the end of the street, he turned, traversing the road that paralleled Eliana's backyard. Acres and acres of cornfields provided no easy access in or out. She'd be safe.

Wouldn't she? One night would tell him a lot.

Fremont was a small town by most standards, though the population of about twenty-seven thousand provided full amenities. Like decent accommodations. Riker turned onto Main Avenue and spotted the sign for an established chain hotel a mile from Eliana's neighborhood.

He pulled into the lot and parked near the front doors, contemplating his options. He wasn't disobeying Beckham's orders. His commander had simply said the cabin might be a good place for Riker to go. Technically, he only had to stay out of the investigation. If the Nites dared to show up here, Nelson would notify him, and Riker would respond immediately.

From here. And if the night proved uneventful, he'd travel to the cabin first thing in the morning.

Reassured of his plan, he climbed out of the truck and released Ammo. Hauling his bag, he walked to the front desk to secure a first-floor room.

Even if Eliana's program served as a catalyst for condemning him to prison for a murder he didn't commit, he couldn't bear the thought of someone hurting her.

Eliana peered out of her office window. A soft breeze fluttered the lace curtain, dispelling the stuffiness. She spotted Officer Nelson's police cruiser parked on the street in front of her house. A text from him dinged on her phone.

Doing okay?

She smiled and typed.

Yes.

Holler if you need anything.

Will do.

She waved and let the curtain close. Night had fallen and since the time Riker had left hours before, nothing bad had happened.

Proof she didn't require police protection.

Still, having the officer outside provided a measure of comfort. Riker and Commander Walsh were wrong. The earlier attack had simply been a senseless drive-by shooting. It might not have even been aimed at her personally but could have been someone upset with one of the businesses in that area. Assured of her reasoning, she lifted her favorite pink mug and sipped sweetened oolong tea. She fed her nervous energy by popping three potato chips in her mouth, relishing the salty treat. If she had to work on this case much longer, she might need to resort to eating celery or she'd pick up unneeded pounds quickly.

The clock on her laptop screen read 11:25 p.m. Eliana

dropped into her desk chair and studied the computer code she'd nearly memorized.

Planted evidence wasn't an unreasonable theory, and it explained Riker's DNA inside the glove, thereby producing the composite sketch. So why did her instincts say something wasn't right?

"Whose side am I on?" she mumbled aloud.

Eliana pushed away from her desk and stood, pacing a short path. "Lord, I need wisdom here. I tout my belief in unbiased investigations, and now I am trying to disprove my program for Riker's sake." No. Not negate the results, explain, and with solid proof, justify them.

Was she biased to the truth because she didn't want Riker to be guilty? What if he had really killed Moneyman?

And then what? She'd bear the burden of responsibility for Riker's incarceration. The team would surely embrace her into the fold then, right? Not. Ugh. Eliana slid back into the chair and rested her head on the cool glass desktop, unable to deny her heart.

She cared about Riker…and she believed he was innocent.

Then rely on science. Eliana sat up and pored over her computer coding in search of a reasonable explanation for the sketch's resemblance. Combined with the strange evidence, her confusion only mounted. When her eyes burned and her vision blurred, she logged out of the program and turned off the lights.

She entered her bedroom where the breeze had grown stronger, wafting in the sweet scent of impending rain and fluttering the lace curtains. Without air-conditioning, her house needed the refreshing coolness. Besides, the window faced the street where the kind officer watched over her. Riker's instructions to keep the house locked up bounced to the forefront of her mind and she closed the window and secured the lock.

Maybe after a few hours of sleep, the answer to Riker's dilemma would come to her. Flipping off her lamp, she snuggled down between the crisp cotton sheets and allowed her mind to consider her ex-boyfriend. His touch, like a battery voltage, had awakened her senses and her heart. Though he'd not asked, and she'd not offered, he deserved to know why she'd left school and never told him goodbye. But how could she reveal that without telling him about her past and Hunter's death? The information would only add to his already antagonistic attitude and Riker would think she'd used him to endorse PHACE for her own benefit, which, technically, she had. She'd been honest about her goal, just not her motive.

Her thoughts transitioned to Riker and she closed her eyes, only to have an idea spring them open again. Eliana reached for her cell phone, activating her favorite voice recording app.

"Perhaps the answers lie in the coding anomalies?" She set the phone down, determined to tackle it first thing in the morning. Satisfied she had a plan, she surrendered to sleep.

A boom and crackling jolted Eliana awake.

Lightning flashed, illuminating an intruder's hooded face as he hovered over her, wielding a gun. He pressed the barrel hard against her forehead. "You should've stayed out of it."

Eliana thrust her hands upward, striking the man's hand away and catching him off guard. Then she kicked with all her might, hitting her intended mark. He gasped and bent over.

She scrambled for the edge of the bed, but he clamped her ankles in a powerful hold, dragging her backward. "Help—" Eliana's plea burrowed into the mattress as the intruder shoved her face down, attempting to smother her.

Stars danced before her eyes as she fought for air.

The distant sound of thunder boomed.

She tucked her legs and managed to get them under her, then jerked upright, headbutting the intruder.

He released his hold momentarily, but he was fast, clamping down again and yanking her closer to him.

Eliana flung her arms wide, grazing the books on her nightstand with her fingers. She clutched the first hardback and twisted, flinging the book hard, and struck him. Jumping off the bed, she landed with a thud on the hardwood floor.

The storm raged outside, casting flashes of light into the room.

He cut her off, blocking her exit. The intruder wavered, obviously still in pain.

In her peripheral, she spotted her open closet door.

"Help!" Thunder drowned out her cry.

Praying against reality that Officer Nelson heard her anyway, she dove for the closet.

A bullet hit the frame, spraying wood just as she whipped the door shut.

Eliana ripped a scarf off the hook and tied it around the knob, then pulled tight and dropped to sit, feet braced on either side of the doorframe.

Her chest heaved with fear and adrenaline.

Dread that she'd die before rescue arrived, she bowed her head. *Oh, God, please help me!*

The storm continued to rage, rattling the house with booming thunder. A flash of lightning illuminated two black boots at the one-inch gap between the door and floor.

"You can't hide in there forever!" The man rattled the knob, nearly ripping Eliana's arm out of the socket as they played a deadly game of tug-of-war.

The door stilled, and his footfalls faded.

The storm rumbled the atmosphere.

Eliana waited, listening. No other sounds. Had he given up? Left? Was Officer Nelson coming?

Hands shaking, she didn't relinquish her hold on the scarf.

She scooted closer, watching the space for any signs of movement.

Only slivers of shadows appeared on the floor. Rain pelted hard against the house.

Had the intruder gone?

In rapid fire, bullets impaled the door with hissing *pffts*. Eliana scurried to the side to avoid being shot.

She clung to the scarf.

The gunshots stopped.

Eliana leaned her forehead on her outstretched arms, still clinging to the silk fabric.

Unwilling to move, she waited. Listening.

When she'd counted to a hundred, twice, she slowly released the scarf. Her old softball bat stood in the corner and Eliana grasped it. Weapon in hand, she got to her feet and gripped the knob, careful not to move it too quickly. Sucking in a fortifying breath, she turned the knob with slothlike motion. Inch by painfully slow inch, she pushed the door open enough to peer through a slit.

The room was dark, and the hallway loomed ahead.

She took a step. The betraying floorboards creaked, resounding in her ears, and announcing her presence.

Eliana froze, clutching the bat in both hands. She shifted toward the opening and used the tip of the bat to push the door wider.

A bullet pinged off the steel.

She screamed and ducked.

The intruder flung open the door, and Eliana swung the bat, striking the man.

He stumbled backward.

Eliana's second swing connected with his jaw, jolting his face sideways with a sickening snap accompanied by the heavy thud of the gun hitting the floor and skidding away.

Another strobe of lightning flashed in the room.

She lunged, but a tackle from behind sent Eliana flying forward. She landed chin-first on the hardwood. Pain exploded up her face.

Air whooshed from her lungs.

The force thrust the bat from her hands and it toppled on the hardwood, out of reach.

The man released her, stood, then kicked her in the ribs, cutting off her next scream. "No one will help you!"

She gasped and rolled into the fetal position.

Clutching her hair, he yanked Eliana's head back. She reached for his hand, desperate to free his hold, but he gripped tighter. Then a click and the cold steel of a blade touched her neck.

She froze.

Fight. The word floated to her in a war cry.

The distant sound of thunder boomed.

"Your cop isn't coming."

She blinked. Riker? Eliana stretched out her fingers, grazing the cord that dangled from her bureau. She clamped down and tugged with all her strength. Her favorite gaudy porcelain lamp came down with a thud, crashing on the assailant and startling him. His switchblade clattered to the floor.

Eliana rolled to her back and thrust her feet upward, landing squarely on the man's stomach. He spewed an oomph and accompanying curse.

She spotted the gun, only a foot away. Scurrying to her knees, she dove for the weapon, wrapping her fingers to secure it. She turned and lifted the pistol at the attacker.

His hands flew up protectively. "No!"

She aimed and, squeezing her eyes shut, fired. The force thrust the gun upward, startling Eliana.

Fast footfalls stomped on the wood floorboards, growing fainter, and she opened her eyes.

Emboldened by his fleeing, she chased after the attacker. But he disappeared out the back door and into the pouring rain.

Eliana slammed the door and secured the lock. Then she flipped on every light as she rushed to her room and grabbed her cell phone off the nightstand. She dialed Officer Nelson while peering out of the window. The rain poured in sheets, eliminating her view of the car parked in front of the house. Why wasn't he answering? Why hadn't he come to her rescue?

Eliana called Riker and he answered on the first ring. "What's wrong?"

"A man attacked me. Officer Nelson isn't responding. I have a bad feeling."

"Is his car there?"

"Yes, but the rain is blocking my view of him from my window." She rambled, not giving Riker a chance to respond, "I think he's hurt. The man said my 'cop isn't coming.' What did that mean?"

"Stay inside! Lock the doors. Call 9-1-1. I'm on my way."

Without replying, she nodded as though Riker would see her.

"Now!"

"Okay." She prayed the attacker wouldn't return. Eliana slid down the wall, dialing 9-1-1 and adding a prayer for Officer Nelson.

"What's your emergency?" the dispatcher asked.

"Help. We need help." Eliana spewed her address then rambled the details of the attack. Her pulse drummed, drowning out the dispatcher.

"Ma'am? Who is with you?"

"Nelson. Officer. He's outside."

"Is he hurt?"

Eliana blinked and rose, peering out the window. "I don't... I don't know."

"I'm sending help. Stay on the phone with me." The dispatcher rattled instructions, but Eliana dropped the device into her pajama shorts pocket. She snagged her robe off the bedroom door hook and slipped it on, securing the sash around her waist.

In a daze, she moved toward the front door. The dispatcher's question lingered. What if the attacker had hurt Nelson? Rescue was coming. Was he scared and crying for help? Like Hunter had done, dying alone because no one responded in time?

With the intruder's weapon in hand, Eliana made her way outside and down the front steps. *God, please make me brave.*

The wind whipped, pelting rain into her eyes, blurring her vision. She moved slowly, wielding the gun for protection, then hurried to the cruiser's driver's door.

Eliana gasped.

Fragmented glass covered the floor and seat. The radio had a hole in it, confirming the shooter had made sure Nelson couldn't call for help.

He was gone!

FOUR

Lightning splintered the sky, startling Eliana. She spun, gun in hand, and surveyed the surrounding inkiness. Was the killer watching her or had he gone? A gust of wind whipped her hair around her face and she slapped away the strands. Sprinting through pools of water that formed on the street and sidewalk, she bounded for the safety of her home. Another flash of lightning halted her in place, drawing attention to the darkened figure sprawled in her side yard.

Eliana recognized Nelson's light uniform before she reached him. He lay facedown in the grass.

Unmoving.

She scanned the area, but seeing no one, shifted the gun to one hand and reached for Nelson's neck with the other. Her fingers probed his wet flesh, searching for a pulse. There! She paused, praying she'd not imagined the delicate movement beneath her fingers.

Dread swarmed her, and a shiver snaked down her back like the rain soaking her clothing and hair. Eliana stood, gun in hand, and guarded. Eerie silence mingled with the raging storm, and she visually roved the yard for any sign of the assailant. In a cautious pivot, she studied the darkened tree line to her right, her gaze traveling upward to where the branches and leaves canopied overhead.

Muffled murmurs of a woman's voice reminded Eliana that her phone was inside her short's pocket. She shifted the gun and retrieved the device, pressing it to her ear. "Are you still there?"

"Yes," the dispatcher replied. "What's—"

"Send an ambulance! He's hurt!"

"Describe his injuries."

Veiled by the storm and night, Eliana couldn't see details, and Nelson's uniform was soaked. "I can't tell. It's too dark out here. But Officer Nelson is hurt." She couldn't bring herself to say he was dead. *Please don't be dead.* "Please hurry!"

At the mention of his name, Nelson coughed.

Unable to hold the phone and gun and help the officer, Eliana opted to drop the device. It landed with a soft thud in the grass. The storm consumed the dispatcher's voice. Eliana worked to heave Nelson over, but his immense frame made the efforts difficult. Finally, she rolled him onto his side and transitioned Nelson into the recovery position she'd learned in her first-aid class. Leaning closer to his mouth, she exhaled relief at the shallow breaths that tickled her ear. "I'm here. Hold on."

Eliana kept the gun and surveyed the area, aware the killer might be watching them. Unwilling to leave Nelson alone, she prayed. "Lord, hide us and please bring help soon." Eliana rubbed the officer's shoulder as he labored to breathe. "I'm here, Nelson. Help is coming. Hold on."

Riker's heart stalled in his chest at the sight of Nelson's patrol car. Slowing his pace, he swept the flashlight beam over the vacant interior, where shattered glass covered the seat and a hole pierced the radio.

"Eliana?" His voice blended with the thunder. With Ammo at his side, Riker rushed to the front door. "Eliana!"

"Here! Help!" Her desperate cry reached him from the side of the house.

He jumped down the porch steps and ran around the house, where Eliana knelt beside Nelson's body.

Eliana waved at him then she jumped to her feet. "Riker, help!"

His eyes fixated on the gun in her hand as he sprinted to her, the flashlight beam bouncing across the lawn. "Put down the gun!"

She blinked, arms raised, and glanced at her hand as though seeing the pistol for the first time. She gently set the gun on the ground.

"Sit." Riker tugged on the leash and Ammo dropped to a sit. "Is he—"

"He's alive!" A flash of lightning illuminated the blood that marred her arms and hands.

"Are you hurt?" Riker visually inspected her.

"No." She knelt again, comforting Nelson.

Sirens shrieked in the distance, promising help.

Riker squatted beside her. "Where did you get a gun?"

"The intruder!" Eliana jerked to look at him. "We fought, and he dropped it, so I grabbed it and shot at him."

Riker twisted, scanning the house. "The shooter is dead in your house?"

"No, he got away."

Riker pressed two fingers against Nelson's neck. His own pulse drummed in his ears. "Please, God. Please." The faintest hint of movement had him exhaling relief and gratitude.

He examined Nelson for injuries and winced at the crimson circles staining his light brown uniform. The entrance wounds appeared in the space above Nelson's bulletproof vest near his trapezius muscles. No exit wounds meant the bullets remained inside his body.

His friend gasped, and Riker dropped the flashlight.

"I'm here." His throat constricted. "Fight, Nelson! Help is coming."

Thunder roared above, pierced by the scream of sirens on the street. Red and blue lights strobed the night sky and the backdrop of lightning daggers splintered above.

"Eliana, please go tell the rescue team where we are," Riker instructed.

She jumped to her feet and disappeared around the house.

Ammo whined, and he stroked the dog's damp fur. "I know, buddy."

Within seconds, officers rushed to them.

"He's got multiple gunshot wounds," Riker hollered over the storm.

The first responder dropped to her knees beside him and reached for her shoulder mic, reporting the information. "EMTs are right behind us." She touched Nelson's neck. "Faint pulse, but he's got one."

Riker didn't move, unwilling to release his friend until the paramedics arrived. Eliana placed a hand on his shoulder.

"What happened?" the second officer asked.

"A man attacked me in my home." Wet tendrils framed Eliana's face. "I didn't see his face before he ran out of my house."

"Did you hear shots fired?"

"No, the sound was muffled," Eliana answered.

Riker studied the gun, fit with a silencer, lying in the grass. "You said the intruder used that gun?"

Eliana nodded and explained to the officer that she'd taken the weapon during a fight.

"That's impressive," he replied. "I'll have it logged into evidence." A third officer approached and began documenting the evidence.

"Any sign of the shooter?" the female officer asked.

Riker shifted into cop mode. "None."

"Someone saw this guy!" She addressed her cohorts. "Establish a perimeter and cordon off this section. Have Oslow canvass the area and start interviewing neighbors."

"Talk to everyone," the male officer added.

Finally, two paramedics sprinted to them.

"Multiple gunshot wounds," one officer reported.

"Let's get him out of there," the first paramedic said. "Sir, please move out of the way."

"We lost his pulse," her partner advised, shifting to perform CPR.

Riker got to his feet and Eliana prayed softly, "Lord, help him."

After several chest compressions, the medic checked Nelson's pulse and announced, "We're back!"

"Eliana, please take Ammo so I can help them with Nelson." Riker passed her the leash then assisted the paramedics in loading Nelson onto the stretcher. Together, they carried his friend out to the rig on the street. The female paramedic slid in beside Nelson and the male ran to the driver's seat. They roared away from the scene. Frozen in place, Riker watched until the ambulance's lights faded from sight. His arms hung like weights on either side of his body. The sweet fragrance of rain mingled with the copper scent of blood. "How did this happen?"

"He's going to make it, right?" Eliana stood beside him, eyes welling with tears.

Without thinking, he pulled her into an embrace, needing her touch. She melted against his chest, wrapping her arms tightly around him.

"Yes. He will." Riker struggled to swallow. "Nelson's a fighter." *Lord, he'll require a miracle to survive those wounds.*

"Marshal? Ma'am?" An older officer approached. "I'm sorry, but I need to get your report."

Riker blinked the rain from his eyes. "Let's go inside."

They made their way up the sidewalk, passing two officers who encircled Nelson's unit with yellow crime scene tape to cordon off the area. The unrelenting storm persisted, pouring water in sheets.

"Give me a second." Riker released Eliana, missing her touch instantly. "Go on ahead, I'll catch up." She nodded and he sloshed through the puddles to Nelson's car. He reached in and flipped on the overhead light, immediately spotting the glimmer of an AR round on the passenger's-side floorboard. "Found something." He pointed to the round, then rose and surveyed the neighborhood.

With the multitude of mature trees, the shooter had no lack of hiding places. Had he lured Nelson away from his cruiser then shot out the radio so he couldn't call for help? Or had he shot at the car before realizing Nelson wasn't inside?

A silencer combined with the storm's disguise explained why Eliana hadn't heard gunfire. He hurried to catch up with the officer gently guiding Eliana and Ammo toward her house. Riker joined them as they entered her living room, but he paused by the door, aware his clothes and shoes soaked the tile floor. Eliana schlepped to her couch and sank onto the white cushions. Clearly, she was in shock, and Riker longed to pull her into his arms. Ammo rushed to his side and he hesitated, unsure how to proceed. They were drenched and dripping water on the floor.

As if sensing his unease, Eliana got to her feet. "I'll get you a towel." She disappeared into the hallway.

"I'm Sergeant Usher." The officer's gaze said he already knew Riker's identity, but he saw no judgment, only mutual respect.

"US deputy marshal Riker Kastell and my K-9, Ammo." He deliberately refrained from referring to his dog as *retired*.

"Nelson spoke highly of you," Usher replied.

Riker looked down, forcing his emotions to the floor.

Eliana reappeared, dressed in dry clothes and carrying towels, which she passed to Riker. He busied himself mopping up the mess, then dried off Ammo before stepping off the tile. Eliana had returned to her seat on the sofa. "I just need a minute, please."

"Of course," Usher said.

Riker led Ammo to the recliner chair across from Eliana and motioned for the dog to sit, but Ammo strained toward the sofa. He released the leash, allowing his K-9 to go to Eliana's side. Riker snagged a crocheted afghan off the back of the recliner and wrapped Eliana in its warmth before sitting on the opposite end of the couch. He noticed the way her hands shook as she tugged the blanket tighter. Ammo scooted closer to Eliana, resting his head on her lap.

She glanced down and gave him a shaky smile. "Hey, handsome." Extending her hand, she stroked the dog's damp fur, and he closed his eyes in appreciation.

The tender exchange touched Riker and he couldn't help but feel a little jealous at the way Ammo instinctively understood how to comfort Eliana.

The officer who'd worked on cordoning Nelson's unit burst through the front door. "Officer Usher, I'd like to assist in here, if that's okay?" He approached Riker, extending his hand. "Marshal, my name is Vance Steller."

Riker returned the gesture. "Riker Kastell."

"Nelson was my FTO," Steller said, referencing the title of field training officer.

"The entire department and most of the surrounding counties are looking for this shooter," Usher interjected. "Everyone loves Nelson."

Riker appreciated that they all spoke of his friend in the present tense. Nelson would survive. He swallowed the emotional wedge in his throat. "He's an amazing man. My team is also on the way from Omaha to assist."

"We'll find who did this," Usher assured him, glancing at Eliana. He moved to squat in front of her. "Ma'am, I'm Sergeant Yale Usher. Nelson is a dear friend, so first, I want to say thank you for staying with him." The older man's voice quavered a bit, but he quickly regained control. "Second, I want to find who did this. So, everything you tell me is important. Even if it seems minuscule."

Eliana nodded. "I last texted with Nelson a little after eleven o'clock, then I went to bed." She turned to face Riker, eyes wide. "He was parked in front of my house and I locked the windows."

He squeezed her forearm reassuringly. "You did nothing wrong."

"The thunder and lightning storm must've woken me up. When I opened my eyes, the guy was standing over me with a gun," Eliana said.

Usher took notes as she tearfully recounted the entire incident. He spoke expertly, extracting details of the event. Riker appreciated the way he maintained a calm composure while Riker's own emotions warred within him. Eliana's voice quivered as she answered Usher's questions, and her vulnerability nearly undid him. He never should've left her. Her detailed account stunned him, and with each word, rage and guilt battled within him. Why hadn't he stayed and helped? He tensed, fury boiling his blood at Eliana's description of the man attacking her. He would find this maniac and make sure he never tasted freedom again.

"The other officer took the intruder's gun." Eliana clarified how she'd fought back and picked up the weapon, sending the attacker fleeing.

Riker stared in amazement. She'd not only fought for her life, but she'd also retaliated at the assailant with his own gun, and then cared for an injured officer. "You're amazing," he said. Was it possible they had Moneyman's murder weapon?

"Marshal Kastell found an AR round inside Nelson's unit," Steller noted.

"He used an automatic rifle to shoot Nelson," Riker added.

Steller radioed the information into Dispatch. "I'll follow up on the ballistics."

"My team member, Skyler Rios, is a great resource. I'll text you her information." The men swapped phone numbers and Riker sent a message to the team with a quick update. If the gun matched Moneyman's murder, they'd have a huge lead and possibly fingerprints.

When Usher finished taking the report, Steller said, "I'll get my kit." At Riker's quirked eyebrow, he explained. "I'll start in the back rooms and work my way up here. We don't have a designated evidence recovery team, so we do the work."

He nodded. Many small departments couldn't afford the personnel dedicated to crime scene investigation, so they trained their officers to handle it.

"Nelson was ex-military," Riker said. "This guy had to have caught him off guard. The AR round I found inside his unit was shot from a distance, possibly in the trees, using a scope."

"The wind and rain account for the missed trajectory," Usher added.

"Nelson never would've allowed someone to approach." Riker walked to the window and glanced out. "The storm is lessening. Ammo's a trained tracker. We'll search and see if there's any evidence of the shooter's presence."

"Might be hard to find with the mud and moisture," Usher contended.

"Possibly." Riker shrugged. "But I'd like to try."

A text from Walsh dinged on his cell phone: ETA 15.

"My commander will be here soon."

"Excellent. I'll bring him up to speed," Usher said.

"Thank you." Ammo tilted his head, watching Riker. "Ready to work?" In response, the dog's thumping tail told Riker all he needed to know. "Come." Ammo rushed to his side, and he glanced at Eliana. "Please stay here with Officer Usher."

She nodded, pulling the afghan tighter around her.

Riker and Ammo made their way out the back door and into the yard. The rain had calmed to a sprinkle and the thunder's distant low rumble indicated the storm had expelled its fury, moving the system out of town. As they neared the side of the house, Riker glanced at the street where officers lingered around the property. Several still spoke with neighbors across the street, working the scene.

Riker knelt in front of Ammo and, using hand gestures to emphasize his instructions, said, "Hunt."

The grass was wet, so locating signs of the intruder wouldn't be easy, but he couldn't stand by and do nothing.

Ammo surprised him by striding toward the trees that bordered Eliana's backyard. The dog paused, nose lifted, then continued forward. He repeated the actions through the tree line and along the creek. Ammo strained against his leash, forcing Riker to jog to keep up with him.

They weaved through the trees paralleling the creek to where a single plank of wood leaned against the opposite side of the bank. Most of the wood was submerged beneath the water, providing proof of the intruder's escape path. Beyond the water, the land spanned into acres of cornstalks. Eyes fixed on the field, Riker was unprepared when Ammo spun, nearly yanking his arm out of the socket. Lunging and snarling, Ammo tugged Riker back to the trees just as a whiz and *pfft* blazed past Riker's cheek. He ducked and rushed for cover in the foliage.

Peering around a large, low-hanging branch, Riker glanced out.

Another shot pierced the trunk beside him, spraying fragments of bark.

He ducked again, holding Ammo close. Several more shots pinged around them. Staying low, Riker lifted his gun and returned fire in the direction he assumed the man was hiding. With the darkness and the corn growth, spotting the shooter was impossible.

Riker spun and sprinted with Ammo toward Eliana's yard. They passed her house and rushed to the street where the officers were vigorously working the scene. "Active shooter!" Officers appeared from all directions and Riker rapid-fired the information. "He's in the cornfield opposite the creek! Most likely has a scope AR."

The officers took off through the yard. Riker and Ammo went to the back door, and spotted Eliana standing at the kitchen window. Her dazed look seemed fixed beyond him.

What was she doing?

She'd be an open target for the shooter.

Gunshots exploded.

Riker bolted for the back door. "Eliana! Get down!"

Eliana ducked, splashing water across the counter and onto the floor. Riker and Ammo burst inside, slamming the door. "Stay down."

"Were those gunshots?" Eliana reached overhead for the hand towel on the counter. She dried her hands while the warm water she'd relished only seconds before ran from the faucet.

"Yes." Riker closed the window blinds and shut off the spout. "I didn't mean to scare you, but you were an easy target standing there."

Officer Usher ran in from the living room, gun drawn. "I heard on the radio."

"The shooter is still out there." Riker gestured to the backyard. "He nearly killed us! If Ammo hadn't warned me, we'd be dead."

"Did you see him?" Usher moved to the door.

"No. He hid in the cornfield and must've used a scoped AR."

"AR?" Eliana asked, still crouching by the kitchen sink.

"ArmaLite rifle," Usher replied, reaching for his shoulder mic. "Status update?" His radio blared to life with replies as he bolted outside.

"You can get up," Riker said.

Eliana slowly rose. "He's still here?"

"I don't know. With all the cops around here, he probably bolted," Riker said.

From her position in the kitchen, she surveyed the living room, separated by a half wall and archway. "Are we safe in here?"

"If he can't see us, he can't shoot us," Riker answered. "Let's move to the couch."

She led the way, dropping onto her sofa. Eliana longed to wash away the nightmarish events that replayed in her mind on an endless reel, but her thoughts hovered on Nelson. She bowed her head, lifting her voice and heart to God. "Lord, please save Nelson."

Riker put a hand on her shoulder. "Amen."

She met his eyes and a knowing glance passed between them.

"Ammo, down." He accompanied the command with a flattened palm, and the dog obediently dropped to a sphinx pose beside her.

Riker walked to the living room and peeked out the side of the blinds.

"Are you both okay?" Eliana scanned man and dog for any injuries.

"Yeah." He faced her. "I can't believe how nervy this

guy is, considering the number of officers surrounding this area."

"You said Ammo saved you?"

"He must've detected the guy tromping around in the corn and lunged. If he hadn't pulled me when he did, the shot the guy fired off would've hit me in the head." He crossed the room and sat beside her, stroking the dog's ears. "Thanks for saving my life, buddy."

Eliana put her head in her hands, overwhelmed by the magnitude of the events. Riker's presence brought comfort, though she'd prefer to throw herself into his arms. Instead, she bowed her head again to pray.

Riker's cell phone interrupted her petitions. "Yes, sir." He got to his feet and hurried to open the front door.

Beckham stepped inside. "Didn't want you to shoot me if I just walked in." The comment was no doubt meant to lighten the mood, but Eliana's emotions were raw and she couldn't bring herself to smile. He frowned and quickly shut the door. "The officers are scouting the area."

"They won't find him," Riker said, sliding into the recliner.

"Skylar is working with the Fremont PD on the shooter's weapon and the AR round you found inside Nelson's unit," Beckham informed them.

Eliana faced him, understanding flooding her. "If you can match the ballistics to the bullet fragments from Moneyman, it'll prove Riker isn't the killer."

"It might confirm the pistol is the murder weapon, but doesn't prove who shot it," Riker replied.

"But it will help us," Beckham added.

"Doesn't the shooting prove Riker is innocent?" Eliana asked.

Beckham shook his head. "If only it were that easy."

"It's too bad that death threats aren't enough to get the charges removed," Riker replied.

"But it helps, right?" Eliana asked.

"Depends on how the prosecution spins it," Riker said. "They could argue that I made the whole attack appear as though someone was out to kill me, when in fact, it was my partner trying to silence me before I outed him."

"Not to mention you were here with Eliana earlier, so you knew the layout of the house and could've broken in," Beckham added.

"Thanks for that," Riker mumbled sarcastically.

"Just posing the viable argument," Beckham replied.

Eliana groaned. "I hadn't even considered that option."

"My instincts say the answer lies in your program," Beckham said. "This has developed into more than the Nites trying to stop Eliana from testifying. There's something in the composite that the killer doesn't want us to find." He turned to face her. "Have you made any progress in figuring out why PHACE created Riker's sketch?"

With both men's gazes fixed on her, Eliana swallowed hard. Loath to confess the truth, she fixed her eyes on Ammo's brindle fur.

"Did you run the second sample?" Beckham pressed.

Eliana nodded, still unwilling to look at them.

"And?" Riker injected.

"And…" She looked up. "I got the same results."

Beckham grumbled something unintelligible under his breath. "But we know it's not Riker, and the fact that this maniac is still trying to kill him proves that." His phone rang, interrupting their conversation. "I need to take this." Beckham moved to the kitchen, his voice low. He returned, wearing a frown, and tucked his phone into his jacket. "The team is stuck behind a major accident that has blocked traffic in both directions on the highway. They're trying to take a detour route, but it's delaying their arrival."

"Of course they are," Riker mumbled. "Considering most of north central Nebraska's law enforcement is out searching for the shooter, I'm not sure it'll make a difference. This guy's propensity to disappear is alarming."

The creak of the back door interrupted the conversation. Riker spun around, snagged his gun from his hip holster, and moved around the corner with Ammo at his feet, barking.

"It's just me, Usher," a voice called.

"Had to make sure." Riker lowered his weapon. Then to Ammo, he motioned and said, "Down."

Officer Usher entered the living room. "Wherever he was, he got away."

"Case in point," Riker said. "He just vanishes."

Usher quirked an eyebrow at Eliana and she shrugged. He approached Beckham with an outstretched hand, introducing himself, but her focus remained on Riker. Why was he acting so strangely?

"We're going to remove Eliana from the premises and secure her in a safe house," Beckham advised Usher.

The officer nodded. "I'll make sure units provide you a safe departure from the city."

"We appreciate that," Beckham said.

"Wait a minute." Eliana stood. "I haven't agreed to go anywhere."

"Sir, I'll update my officers while you all work out the details," Usher said, excusing himself and hurrying out the front door.

"The intruder following us here is disconcerting," Eliana admitted.

"Tell me about it," Riker said with a sigh. "I watched for tails. How did he find us?"

"With Eliana's name on the news, it wouldn't have taken a rocket scientist to track down her address," Beckham answered. "I never should've allowed you to come back here."

Eliana bristled. "As much as I appreciate your concern

for me, no one allowed me to do anything. This is my home and my life. I have a right to say where I will and will not go."

As if she were invisible and had not spoken, Riker continued his conversation with Beckham. "Eliana cannot stay here."

"I agree," Beckham said, leaning against the wall. "We'll up the detail and move her to a safe house."

Her fast reaction sent pain blasting through her neck. "What? Wait a minute," Eliana said. "I get to have some say in my life."

"They won't stop," Riker argued. "The Nites are ruthless. Whoever is framing me wants to make sure you're dead, too."

"Which is why the two of you need to remain together."

Eliana shook her head. "Absolutely not."

"No way," Riker said in unison.

Beckham lifted a hand. "I cannot ask another police department to step into this. We're equipped to handle the Nites. We can't sacrifice another team member to guard Eliana," Beckham continued. "Since you can't work your own case, Riker, it stands to reason you can provide the detail. I'm on board with giving you the assignment now. Two birds and all that."

Riker seemed to study her. Eliana's cheeks warmed under his probing gaze. Could she handle being in his company for an extended period? The man made it clear he wasn't her biggest fan. Did she really want to be stuck with him? The thought of the intruder invading her home and the battle that ensued solidified her resolve. She'd take Riker's cranky attitude for the safety of protection. No one else was capable. Nelson was proof.

"Sir, can I speak with you privately?" Riker asked.

"We're not discussing this any further," Beckham answered. "Eliana, please gather your personal items for a lengthy stay."

Riker's life depended on her deciphering the coding. Either enough to place reasonable doubt or to figure out why the results presented the way they did. Eliana surveyed her small house. It wasn't fair the killer had driven her from her own home. And yet she couldn't disagree the danger was mounting.

"Eliana," Riker said, his voice low and husky. It sent shivers up her back that had nothing to do with the fear. The way he looked at her made Eliana come alive and, as much as she couldn't surrender to those feelings, there was no other option.

"You assured me Nelson could handle my protection detail," Eliana argued. "And the killer still found a way to not only get to me, but he nearly killed Nelson!"

Riker's eyes darkened. "I can't disagree with her there. Nelson was a trained professional, both military and law enforcement. She's right."

Beckham heaved a sigh. "What do you suggest?"

Riker paced a small area. "Put her in one of the team's custody. I don't mean to sound arrogant, but let's be real. We're the only ones capable of protecting Eliana. How about Skyler? She's got Bosco to help. Or Tiandra?"

"Negative," Beckham said.

"No offense, but PHACE is my program, and my reputation is on the line. I need to work without fearing for my life. It drains the creative juices." Eliana frowned. Why was Riker making this so difficult? "As you have informed me in the past, I'm an independent contractor, so I do not have to comply with your group. I can say no and walk away. It's my life at risk."

Riker pinned her with a glare. "Sometimes, it's not all about you. Nelson has six little girls and a baby on the way."

His words were like a slap across the face. Eliana gasped. "Oh, no." The weight of the information stabbed her heart and her hand flew to her throat. The poor man and his family. "Lord, please heal him."

"I need air," Riker said, storming to the front door.

FIVE

Riker sat on Eliana's porch steps as the multitude of officers from varying jurisdictions and departments worked the scene. An officer-involved shooting brought out law enforcement's dedicated response, and Riker was grateful. But there were far too many people present for him to feel comfortable about sticking around. They needed to get on the road.

As soon as he cooled off. In truth, he wanted to protect her, but they agitated each another. He couldn't waste that energy when he should be focused on his case. *It's not all about you.* His retaliatory comment, like a two-edged sword, pierced him and lingered with the humidity filling the atmosphere. Was his selfishness in wanting to investigate his case blinding him too?

It's my life. Eliana's proclamation unlocked a vault of memories and triggered an unexpected response, drilling deeper than he wanted to go. And now he struggled to relinquish the young love resentment he'd buried and the personal baggage Eliana's high school abandonment burdened upon him. Why did those old feelings arise? Perception was reality, and his was tainted by too many emotions.

Forgiveness is a process, his mother would say.

Apparently, he had more processing to do.

The sight of Nelson's patrol car reminded Riker that his

friend's life hung in the balance. Without a doubt, Moneyman's killer was the same man who'd shot Nelson. The stakes had risen, and Riker had to bring down the criminal. Something he couldn't do with Eliana in tow.

Her reluctance to relocate, though understandable, was irrelevant. The evidence of carnage that protecting her left behind said everything. Did she not understand her stubbornness was a smack in the face to those trying to help her?

With fresh determination, Riker got to his feet. He had to clear his name and find the actual killer. For Nelson's sake, that required Riker to stay focused and shove away distracting and hindering emotions. And he couldn't have Eliana with him.

Or was he seeing things wrong because of the feelings Eliana had awakened in him?

No. He didn't care about her that way anymore. And wouldn't ever again. She'd proved untrustworthy with his heart once. He wouldn't offer her a second opportunity.

The front door opened, refocusing Riker on the present.

Beckham stepped outside. "Ammo's standing guard while Eliana gathers her stuff."

Since his commander favored Eliana, he'd better start with an apology. "I—"

"Don't explain. You've both been put through the wringer."

Riker blinked at the unexpected response. He'd braced for Beckham to bawl him out. Instead, his kindness added to Riker's guilt.

"I need you to dig deeper and serve as her protector."

Riker opened his mouth to argue, but Beckham continued. "Remember, Eliana's a civilian. She's not a warrior like you and me, and you cannot expect her to react as such."

If only that was his issue, but Riker had no interest in

confessing the details of his past. Instead, he nodded. "I'll apologize to her."

Beckham blocked the door, leaning against it. "That was too easy. What's going on?"

So much for the quick escape. "Sir, I need to find this criminal. He nearly killed Nelson and Eliana. He's framing me and it's obvious he's escalating."

Beckham shook his head.

"Please, I get the rules. But I can't sit by and hope it all works out." Riker's hands fisted at his sides. "I feel like I'm crawling out of my skin."

Beckham sighed. "I understand. I really do."

No, sir, you don't. "So, you'll permit me to assist?"

"Negative." Beckham folded his arms over his chest. "I want you cleared of all charges. I cannot do anything to risk that. And I need you to handle Eliana's detail."

"I appreciate the support and confidence, but Tiandra or Skyler would do a better job with Eliana." Riker had to convince Beckham leaving Eliana with him wasn't the right thing.

Beckham's brow creased. "Why?"

Several silent seconds ticked by as Riker contemplated how to respond.

"There are few benefits to aging. And I do mean few..." Beckham began. "But one of them is the discernment that comes from knowing your people. I can read you better than you think. You plan to go off investigating this case and ignoring everything I've said. You don't want Eliana in tow because she'd not only slow you down, but you'd also have to worry about her safety, which means you can't do anything dumb, like you're hoping to do."

Unable to argue, Riker clamped his mouth shut and looked down.

Beckham gave him a sideways grin. "I appreciate your diligence and integrity, and I promise to keep you informed.

And if there's any place you can participate, I'll invite you in without question."

"But—"

"I know you're not a fan, and I remember why you hate technology," Beckham said. "What happened to Practor was a tragedy," he continued, referring to an earlier case. "But in the end, they exonerated him. Ironically, by technology."

"Yeah, the definition of ironic, don't you think?" Riker asked. "And now I'm stuck in the same position."

"Errors happen even in real police work," Beckham said. "Eliana's program might be exactly what we need to break through this. By providing her detail, you're allowing me to free up other assets, thereby working on your case."

Riker considered his commander's words. "I don't want anyone else endangered. Nelson…" His chest tightened. "I understand."

"I'm glad you're on board because Eliana's detail is a nonnegotiable order." Beckham's unwavering gaze ended the discussion.

Riker looked down at his boots, biting his tongue to keep from speaking. They'd prevent him from accessing the crime scenes anyway, so he'd have to rely on the photos from the evidence technicians and search for leads elsewhere.

"I'll update you with Nelson's condition," Beckham promised.

"Thank you." Riker exhaled and reached for the door. "If I'm doing the detail, I pick the location."

"I assume we're thinking the same place."

Riker nodded. "I prefer to leave tonight while we have the cover of darkness. Also, I don't want anyone following us, so we'll need to make alternative travel plans."

"Roger that. However, I want regularly scheduled check-ins." Beckham paused. "I'll have a cruiser follow you."

"Just to the highway." Once the officer turned off, he'd take an exit onto the closest county road.

"Affirmative."

Riker hurried into the house where Eliana sat, stroking Ammo, a small suitcase beside her. She looked up at his entrance and got to her feet. "I need to apologize—"

"No, you don't. It's on me. I was a jerk," he interrupted. He'd treat her with the care of a witness in need of protection and nothing more. No personal feelings would get in the way, and they'd keep their professional boundaries. "You'll need to pack for rugged terrain. No heels."

Without a word, she stood, dragging the suitcase behind her and retreated to the bedroom. She returned with a duffel bag. They proceeded outside, where Beckham waited. "I'll handle locking everything up when the team is finished here."

"Thank you," Eliana replied, a slight quiver in her voice.

A twinge of guilt and Beckham's quirked brow reminded Riker that Eliana was his charge now. He gave a slight nod of understanding and they loaded into the F-150. Once they got onto the open road, they would be safe, and he'd figure out a way to work on his case. Even with her in tow.

With one last glance at her home, Eliana latched her seat belt. When would she be able to return?

Riker slid behind the wheel. The palpable tension between them melded with her own emotions, bouncing between irritation at his attitude and anger at herself for speaking so callously. Of course, he was stressed. The intruder had shot his friend while he was protecting her. Considering Riker didn't like her to begin with, she understood his abrasiveness.

They reached the highway and Eliana couldn't stand the silence anymore. "Where are we going?"

Two beats passed before Riker responded. "Someplace the criminal can't find us."

Eliana tilted her head, staring up into the darkened sky. "The moon?"

His chuckle brought slight relief, despite the seriousness of the situation. "Something like that. No, my cabin. It's practically off the grid, hard to find, and in my brother's name. We'll be safe there."

Eliana spotted the police cruiser in the side mirror. "Will he accompany us the entire time?"

"Only until we get out of Fremont." Riker flicked a glance in the rearview mirror. "I'm sure the shooter is long gone and hiding underground."

"Except?" The lengthy pause caused more concern for Eliana. "Riker, what aren't you saying?"

He focused on the road. "I'm erring on the side of caution."

Her confusion mounted when he turned off the main highway onto a county road and the unit behind them flashed his overhead lights once, before proceeding past.

"We lost him," she quipped.

"We're taking the scenic route." He made another turn and settled into the seat. "My cabin is about four and a half hours away. Get comfortable."

"I'm honored to see your private getaway," Eliana teased, adjusting her position in the seat.

Riker's shoulders visibly stiffened.

What had she said wrong now?

"It wouldn't be my first choice, but we don't have many options."

"Too bad it's dark out and we can't enjoy this exceptional view." She gestured out the window to the unending farmland surrounding them.

"It looks the same for miles. Corn as far as the eye can see." The corner of his lips lifted.

"Wouldn't a highway be faster?"

"This road is less traveled."

Unwilling to continue the polite but surface conversation, she blurted, "Look. As much as I love road-tripping with you and this communication elephant sitting between us, we need to talk."

"Now's not a good time."

She ignored him. "I feel bad and would like to apologize. I upset you and I didn't mean to."

Riker worked his jaw then said, "This is all unfamiliar territory, I get that. But the danger is real, and there are many lives affected by this case."

Eliana blinked. Had she implied she only cared about herself? "I deserved that. But it certainly wasn't what I intended to convey." She crossed her arms over her chest in a protective gesture, feeling vulnerable and embarrassed by her words.

Riker blew out a breath. "I guess we're both on edge."

She nodded and picked at her fingernail polish. "This whole 'dodging danger' world is a little new to me."

"Yeah, Beckham reminded me of that."

Eliana stared at the yellow lines on the road, blurring her vision. Her natural ability to upset Riker seemed rooted in something deeper than her quirky lack of communication skills. But she appreciated having privacy for her secrets and hardly blamed Riker for keeping his own. "Cooperation is to our advantage, so the animosity between us isn't helping."

"True. Neither of us wants to be stuck together."

Ouch.

Riker continued. "We're both professionals. We'll stick to our duties. Nothing more."

She frowned, confused by the comment. "Sure. Professional from here on out. No one besides you and I truly understand the implications of PHACE's results. We're bonded in the quest for the truth."

Was Riker's silence an indicator he mulled over her words?

"You're a smart lady, Eliana Daines."

She did a double take. Had he just complimented her? The guy ran so hot and cold it was hard to keep up with his moods.

"You're right. We both have a lot to lose and gain with PHACE," Riker said, apparently oblivious to her bewilderment. "Whoever killed Moneyman and shot Nelson knows exactly what that something is." He flipped on the air conditioner. "I need to work on my case, and I didn't want to risk your life."

Maybe she'd read him all wrong and he didn't hate her? The moon hung high in the sky and they passed miles of tall cornstalks, illuminating the golden tassels.

"Until I moved to Nebraska, I'd never realized the process corn goes through. I've worked with several people who said their kids detasseled every summer. I'd never heard of such a thing."

"It's the removal of the tassels at the top of the corn," Riker replied.

Eliana was aware of that but didn't want to offend him, so she quietly listened.

"The kids walk the rows, pulling those off."

He didn't elaborate, but Eliana knew detasseling was a form of pollination control used to cross-breed different varities of corn. She scanned the golden tassels waving in the breeze, realizing she knew very little about Riker. "Did you detassel as a kid or are you an expert in all things corn related?" she teased, hoping to lighten the conversation.

"I had other summer activities, but my cousins worked the fields every year and complained until they got their paychecks."

The simple reminder solidified her conclusions about Riker. He'd probably spent his summers at the pool chasing pretty girls. Eliana reassessed their working relationship and shifted into professional gear. The desire to talk to Riker dwindled. They had little in common, except for a killer determined to silence them. She closed her eyes, opting to pass the time snoozing, or at least faking sleep.

An unexpected crash, followed by the pickup slamming down on the passenger's side, jolted her upright. "What's going on?"

Riker yanked the wheel. "We lost a tire!" He fought for control and Eliana dug her fingernails into the leather seat cushion in a weak effort to protect herself.

Metal grinded against the pavement while the back end of the truck fishtailed. Eliana's prayers got stuck on a continuous loop of *Please, God. Please, God.*

Riker expertly maneuvered the truck on to the shoulder before they skidded to a stop.

Eliana's heart pounded through her throat. "What just happened?"

"I'm not sure. Stay here while I check it out." Riker pushed open his door and stepped outside.

Ammo poked his head over the console, resting it beside Eliana's face. "Hey, sweetie." She reached up to stroke his velvety ears. "That wasn't fun."

He whined and retreated to his place in the back seat.

Eliana rolled down her window, permitting a blast of humidity as thick as gravy into the cab. Rows of corn stretched out on both sides of the truck, fading into inky darkness. She shivered with the sensation someone watched her. There wasn't another car or a house in sight. Her imagination was getting away from her. *Stop being silly.* They were in the middle of a county road in the dead of night. Bad phrase.

Riker's door opened.

Eliana startled and screamed.

He peeked in. "What's wrong?"

She pressed her hand against her chest, panting. "You scared the daylights out of me."

"Did you see something?" He turned, surveying the area.

"No. Sorry."

"Thankfully, we lost the passenger's-side back tire."

"Like that's a good thing?"

"If it had been a front tire, we'd probably be dead."

The hairs on the back of her neck prickled at their too close call with death. "Do you have a spare?"

"Yes, but we have a bigger issue." He retrieved a flashlight from the console and stepped out of the truck.

Eliana pushed open her door and glanced at the back seat, where Ammo sat, ears peaked with interest. "Should I let him out for a break?"

"Sure, thanks." Riker's reply emitted from somewhere near the bed of the vehicle.

She released Ammo and secured his leash as she'd seen Riker do.

Riker mumbled something unintelligible and got to his feet. "Unbelievable."

"I'm afraid to ask."

Ammo explored while she scanned the cornstalks. Did one move? No, she was being paranoid.

"How did he get to the truck?" The firm line of Riker's jaw enhanced his handsomeness.

She must be tired. "Who?"

"Whoever did this." He gestured toward the place where a wheel should've been. "He not only loosened the lug nuts, but he also stripped them. We lost everything, and the near-death skid down this road warped the brake rotor. I couldn't put the spare tire on if I wanted to." Riker slammed a hand against the truck.

Ammo rushed to his side and sat, tail wagging and curious. "Sorry, buddy, I'm frustrated." He knelt and stroked the dog's fur.

Satisfied he'd done his K-9 duty, Ammo resumed his exploration to the length his leash permitted.

"But there were cops everywhere at my house," Eliana said. "How did he get to it without being seen?"

"There were too many people. I should've gotten us out of there earlier." Riker paced, lifted his phone and groaned. "And of course we have no reception." He walked to the truck and removed the keys. "We'll have to walk to the main road and hitch a ride, or at least until I can make a call."

Headlights blazed from behind Riker.

"Oh, good! Someone's coming. We've got a ride." She pointed to the vehicle. "I'll grab my computer." Eliana turned and grabbed her bag from the F-150.

Riker was at her side in a second, pulling her into the cornfield. "Go! Run as far as you can!"

She started into the field, struggling with her bag. Riker took it from her. Hand tight on hers, he led her deep into the foliage.

The sound of screeching tires erupted from the road.

"Where are we going?" she whispered, swiping at the leaves that scraped her skin.

"As far from the truck as you can get."

The hard stalks snapped around her, scratching her arms and face. Eliana stumbled over the uneven ground, forcing her legs to move faster. Ambient light from the moon provided a limited visual of the path and the plant growth disguised them.

Silence danced with the chirrups of crickets.

Rapid gunfire tore through the night.

Riker increased his pace then tugged her to the right. They hurried deeper into the field.

Blasts continued around them, echoing from every direction.

He stopped, pressing a finger to his lips, and they squatted low. Riker motioned at Ammo and he dropped into a sphinx pose.

Additional gunfire.

Then silence.

Even the crickets had quieted.

Footsteps drew closer, crunching on the hard ground. Was the shooter near or had the sound carried to them?

Riker kept his hand flat, maintaining Ammo's attention.

Eliana prayed he wouldn't bark. Pulse thudding in her ears, she followed Riker's gaze.

The identical rows made it impossible to distinguish where they were. He rose slightly in a bent position before motioning for her to follow. Together they crept through the long, narrow trail.

Eliana glanced over her shoulder, spotting the swaying of the tassels, and sucked in a gasp.

She poked Riker and pointed toward the moving stalks. He nodded, and they shifted between rows, diverting to a different path.

The crunching grew louder, the killer's steps moving faster.

They hurried, weaving through the long lines of corn, angling occasionally to change their route.

Finally, Riker stopped. With a hand gesture, he instructed Ammo to drop to a sit. Eliana inched closer.

Frozen in place, they listened for movement.

Had the killer gone?

SIX

Their labored panting consumed the air, and Riker pressed a finger against his lips. Eliana nodded, quieting her breaths. Their only hope of survival was eluding the killer. And he'd stupidly left his gun in the vehicle.

An engine revved and sped away, allowing them to exhale relief.

"He's gone." Riker released his hold of Eliana's hand. "I cannot believe I forgot I'd put my gun in the console. I always have it on me."

"That's my fault. I distracted you with my computer."

"No. It's on me." He wanted to slap himself upside the head for making a rookie mistake.

"How did he find us? And why give up?"

"Good questions. My guess is something scared him away or he's waiting for another opportunity." Riker flipped on the flashlight, illuminating the ground. He led the way, hoping it was correct, but unwilling to convey his concern. Telling Eliana that he wasn't sure where they were in the middle of the cornfield would do nothing to improve her confidence in him.

He swept the beam slowly, retracing their steps by using the crushed stalks for guidance. They walked for what felt like an eternity, finally emerging from the field.

Riker turned. They were several hundred yards from the truck, but at least they'd found their starting point.

In a rush, the trio hurried to the vehicle, and he reached inside. His gun was gone! Riker groaned. "And he's got my weapon."

Eliana's eyes widened. "What do we do now?"

"The only thing we can. Walk until I get some reception to call for help. The truck is out of commission." They were vulnerable in too many ways, and Riker was losing the ability to fake his assurance that all would be fine.

"Roll up the windows and lock the doors. We'll come back for the rest of our things."

"I'm keeping my computer bag." Eliana did as he asked, while Riker surveyed the road. If they went the wrong way, they might walk right into the path of the killer. He prayed there was a farm nearby, but there was no guarantee anyone lived on the property.

"Lord, guide our steps, please."

Eliana jerked to look at him as though he'd spoken in another language. "Why are you looking at me like that?"

"Your prayer surprised me."

With Ammo's leash in hand, they ventured in the opposite direction of the main road. "It's naïve to think we'll get to the cabin without further issue, so I need to establish a few ground rules."

"Like?"

"As you've just experienced, our lives depend on split-second action. In the time it takes me to explain my reasoning, you could die. Please trust me when I say 'go' or 'drop,' or whatever."

"I understand." Eliana kept pace with him. "This can't go on forever, right?"

"The killer assumes we have something on him, or we're getting too close. He won't stop until we're dead."

"I'm confused why he'd frame you and try to kill you. Seems a little erratic."

"I don't have a good answer," Riker replied. "Chasing people through cornfields isn't the Nites's style." At least he hoped not.

"I'm impressed by your ability to navigate us through that maze."

Riker chuckled. "Corn mazes are always a source of autumn entertainment for farm kids."

"Eww. Bugs and all? I barely kept from screeching every time I brushed against something creepy-crawly in there."

"You're not a country girl, I take it?"

"Not even close." Though she'd lived in many places, the country wasn't one of them. Unsure how to respond, Eliana remained silent, their footsteps crunching on the road.

They crested the hill and Riker searched for a signal. "Nothing."

"Should we go toward the highway?"

"No, we'll find a farmhouse soon." He prayed that was true and opted to change topics. "Being out here reminds me of my cousin's farm. I went up for a week every summer until my junior year of high school." Why had he brought that up? He didn't want to discuss their personal issues. Shifting direction, he said, "My grandfather was ill and refused to leave his home." The same house Riker resided in. "So our family took turns caring for him."

"You all rallied to care for him in his house?"

"That's what family does."

"Not all families." Eliana frowned. "That must've been hard."

"It was. He had Alzheimer's and required constant care." Riker sighed. "But in those rare moments, when he was lucid, we had the best talks. He was an amazing man. I miss him all the time."

"Didn't you regret not hanging with your friends at the country club or going on vacations?"

Riker snorted. "Hardly. What gave you that idea?"

She shrugged. "With your beautiful Dundee District house and a cabin in Valentine, I assumed you're wealthy."

She'd pegged him all wrong, although with her classy style, she probably focused on external things. He didn't bother to correct her. His life was none of her business. "Pop needed us and until his death, when I was in college, I loved spending time with him." The memories of his grandfather tore at Riker's heart. "He died young at sixty-four."

"I'm so sorry." They walked along silent for a few seconds before Eliana asked, "Is there a history of Alzheimer's in your family?" She must've caught herself because she quickly added, "Your biological family."

Riker mulled over the question, unsure how much of his private life he wanted to share with her.

"I'm sorry, I shouldn't have asked that. It's none of my business," Eliana said.

Her questions and assumptions had him pondering things he didn't want to focus on. Like the devastating disappointment the murder charges would have on his parents. And the aftermath of going to prison for a crime he hadn't committed. "My mom and dad never hid the fact that I was adopted, but I also had no desire to seek my biological family."

Recalling the summers he'd spent with his favorite grandparent brought a mess of emotions. He'd watched the perfectly healthy, vibrant man he'd adored his whole life slowly lose his battle with a debilitating and wretched disease that stole his mind, faculties and memories.

And both reminders of his precious family rejuvenated his drive to do whatever it took to clear his name. Almost anything. Even if it meant going outside of the law to do it? His heart stalled. Would he? No. He'd fought his whole life for justice. He wouldn't give up or surrender without fighting to the bitter end.

"Is that a light?" Eliana pointed to the east, where a small house stood in the distance.

"What time is it?"

She glanced at her watch. "Five twenty-five."

"We found our farmer." Riker increased his stride, forcing Eliana to walk faster to keep up.

"It's a little early to disturb people."

"The good news is early mornings and late evenings are all part of farm life. That works in our favor. Provided they'll allow us to use a phone."

They hurried toward the lane leading to the white farmhouse. Sure enough, lights glowed from inside.

Once they reached the house, Riker paused beside an old pickup, surveying the space. He spotted a barn and pointed to it. "Stay over there. If I don't return within five minutes, go to the road but stay near the corn so you have a place to hide if necessary. If you see anyone coming, run there for protection and then continue until you get service. Do you have your phone?"

"Yes, but surely there's no harm here."

Riker shot her a glance, hoping she remembered their earlier discussion.

Eliana paused and nodded. "Okay."

"If it's clear, I'll come for you."

"Shouldn't we stay together?"

"If this goes bad, I'd prefer they assume I'm alone. That way, you'll escape." Unless he was walking into a trap.

Riker led Eliana around to the backside of the barn, hiding her from the road and the house. Eliana pulled her computer case beside her and leaned against the wood slats.

"Ammo, guard." Riker gave the corresponding hand signal, and the K-9 maneuvered into position. "If anyone besides me returns, he will attack."

She nodded.

With one last glance over his shoulder, Riker hurried toward the house and up the aged porch steps. He hated that he couldn't see Eliana from where he stood. He'd either hidden her well or left her to die alone.

Eliana shivered, despite the balmy morning air. Ammo had remained on guard. She appreciated his presence, but Riker's absence unnerved her, though she had a good visual of both the house and the road. How long had he been gone?

Ammo's ears rotated like furry radars. Would he hear approaching danger? She shifted behind him, and he glanced in her direction then resumed his guard pose. The stance assured Eliana he'd attack if necessary.

Footsteps crunched on the gravel, drawing closer. Eliana sucked in a breath and flattened herself against the barn wall. Ammo emitted a low warning growl then sniffed the air, tail wagging.

"Just me." Riker rounded the building. "Good job, dude." He praised the dog, who lavished wet kisses on his face. "He acts like I've been gone for days." He chuckled.

Eliana watched in amazement. "He recognized your scent before he ever saw you."

"His hearing is impaired, but his sniffer works fine." Riker got to his feet.

She exhaled relief and passed him Ammo's leash.

"Beckham is on the way. The good news is, we didn't get far from your house, and he was already on the road. Should be here within fifteen minutes."

Eliana gathered the handle of her laptop case and followed Riker off the property. "I told him we'd wait by the pickup."

"No issues borrowing their phone?"

"Not at all. They were very kind. Offered us breakfast, but I declined," Riker replied.

Eliana's stomach growled and her face warmed with embarrassment.

"Maybe I should've accepted." He shot her a sideways grin, revealing his dimples.

"Guess I'm hungrier than I thought." She shrugged.

Riker paused and faced her. "If you're feeling faint or something, I might have a granola bar in my duffel bag."

She shook her head. "No, I'm fine, really."

"Are you sure?"

The genuine concern he showed touched Eliana. She was so used to fending for herself. How long had it been since someone cared enough to even ask if she needed anything? "Thank you, but I can wait until we get somewhere safe."

"Okay, let's put some distance between us and this place before stopping for food," Riker suggested, then resumed walking.

Eliana hurried to meet his pace. "Definitely."

They trailed back the way they'd come, and Riker told her about the kind couple at the farmhouse. As though the earlier terror had never occurred, the sunrise awakened the atmosphere in brilliant shades of purples, pinks and oranges while birds chirped morning songs. True to Riker's prediction, two familiar SUVs approached the disabled F-150, leaning awkwardly on the road.

"Are you up for a short jog?" He gestured to the vehicles.

"Sure. Race you."

"I'll give you a head start and here, let me take that." Riker hefted Eliana's laptop case under his arm like a football, clutching Ammo's leash in the other. "Go!"

Eliana sprinted, but Riker passed her with ease. She increased her pace, using her competitive drive to propel her forward. Riker's long stride outdid her best efforts to catch up. She sidled up to him just as Beckham slid from the driver's side of the first SUV and Skyler Rios emerged from the second.

"You did good," he commended. His voice was steady, as though he'd strolled the distance.

She rolled her eyes and snorted, hand pressed against her chest, trying to catch her breath.

K-9 Bosco hopped out of Skyler's SUV and hurried toward them. Riker released Ammo's leash, allowing the dogs to greet one another.

"Perfect timing," Riker said.

Eliana worked to calm her breathing. Clearly, she was out of shape. In a strange way, she'd enjoyed the challenge, even if he'd beat her.

Skyler shot her a worried look. "Are you all right?"

"Yes," Eliana panted, waving away the concern. "I'm fine."

"Riker." Skyler's scolding tone and icy glare conveyed her disapproval.

He lifted his hands in surrender. "She challenged me."

Eliana laughed. "He's telling the truth."

Skyler shook her head and handed Riker the keys. "Figured you'd prefer a ride with a dog kennel for Ammo. Please bring it back in one piece."

"I'll try," he goaded.

They spoke to one another with the ease of siblings, triggering Eliana's contemplations. A familial connection would explain the results PHACE produced. If only Riker had knowledge of his biological roots.

"We'll stay with the F-150," Beckham said. "Tow truck is en route."

"Shouldn't we stick around?" Eliana asked.

"No. You two need to get on the road as soon as possible," Beckham replied.

"I'll help you transfer your stuff," Skyler suggested, guiding Eliana to the truck. "You're certainly getting more out of this than a beta test for PHACE."

"No kidding. I should've read the fine print in the contract," she joked, studying the F-150. "At first glance, it seems like replacing the tire is all we need."

"Yeah, the criminal kept the appearance normal so the stripped lug nuts would be undetected."

"Whoever is after us is determined to keep us off his trail," Eliana surmised. What if he'd planted evidence to look one way, diverting them from the truth right in front of their faces? PHACE compiled the killer's composite, making him look like Riker, while somehow revealing and hiding the killer's actual identity at the same time. The concept slammed into her, and she turned, facing Riker.

"Are you sure you're all right?" Skyler touched her arm, jolting Eliana to the present.

"Hmm." She addressed the agent. "PHACE developed the composite based on the DNA makeup while concealing something else."

"The answer is hidden within the original crime." Skyler tilted her head.

"Yes." Eliana withdrew her duffel from the back seat, and Skyler carried Riker's bag to her vehicle.

At the far end of the road, Beckham and Riker walked to retrieve the wheel from the ditch.

"He's a little gruff, but a good guy." Skyler leaned against her SUV. "But you knew each other before, right?"

"A long time ago." Eliana hoped she wouldn't ask for more details. "Some aspects of Riker are the same as they were back then."

"And others?"

Eliana surveyed the handsome man, rolling the wheel on the road. He glanced up, catching her, and she averted her gaze.

"Your opinion of Riker matters to him," Skyler said.

Eliana snorted. "Hardly."

Short of her program being the catalyst to send him to prison, she doubted Riker cared what she thought of him.

"There's more below the surface of that handsome exterior," Skyler said with a wink.

Eliana's cheeks warmed. Desperate to conceal her emotions from Skyler, she led the way back to the truck, and peered inside, though there was nothing left to retrieve. "We've got everything," she announced, hoping Skyler hadn't noticed the way Riker affected her.

"His family is close, and he's worried how they'll take this news if/when they find out. They're the most important people in his life." Skyler added, "Do you think he's guilty?"

The question was simple and honest, but answering it was complicated. She longed to be a part of the Heartland Fugitive Task Force, but no matter what PHACE produced, it put her on the wrong side of them. Still, her heart and instincts overrode her ambitions. "No. I don't believe he killed Moneyman."

Skyler nodded and placed a hand on her forearm. "You're in a tough position. But the truth is the only thing that will set Riker free from indictment, conviction or public condemnation. Your program will provide that."

"Or make me enemy number one for your team." Eliana shoved down the emotion accompanying Skyler's kind observation.

"We rely on God's guidance and sovereignty," Skyler replied. "You're not powerful enough to overthrow God."

The simple reminder had Eliana considering the truth. *Lord, forgive me for thinking more highly of myself than I should've. You're in control here. I surrender my will to Yours.* The prayer floated up from her heart, providing a calming peace.

The men loaded the wheel into the bed of the F-150 and Riker hopped in, studying the object.

Eliana and Skyler faced him and moved closer.

"What're you looking for?" Skyler asked, voicing Eliana's internal question.

Riker didn't immediately answer, but his eyes widened, and he removed a small box. "This!" He held up the device, allowing the group to inspect it.

"What is it?" Eliana asked.

"A GPS tracker," Riker said. "He couldn't follow us without being seen, so he waited until we were in a vulnerable position and ambushed us."

"My SUV was at the scene, and Skyler followed me here. However, let's conduct a quick check of both vehicles before you head out," Beckham suggested.

They each took a wheel, searching for other tracking devices.

"Find anything?" Beckham asked.

"I'm not sure what I'm looking for exactly," Eliana admitted. "I don't see anything out of the ordinary."

Riker moved beside her, reinspecting the wheels. "It's clean."

"Funny, if you're not looking for it, you can totally miss what's right in front of your eyes," Skyler said.

"The GPS tracker didn't have flashing lights that declared 'Here I am,'" Riker teased.

Skyler's comment lingered in Eliana's mind, and she studied the agent. What was in front of them that they were missing?

Ammo and Bosco bounded around the vehicles, barking and playing. Impervious to the heaviness of the situation.

"Ah, if only we all lived as carefree as our dogs," Skyler said.

Eliana chuckled. "Yes." She approached the SUV, pausing beside Beckham. "Sir, would it be possible for me to view the crime scene again?"

"The one at your house?" He quirked an eyebrow.

"No, sorry. I meant at Riker's home."

"The team finished a thorough investigation there already," Beckham replied. "What are you looking for?"

"I'm not sure, except I can't help but consider we found what the killer wanted us to find. If that makes any sense."

Beckham nodded, leaning against the SUV. "I agree, but we didn't locate any other evidence."

Riker and Skyler approached. "What are you two conspiring about?"

"Since Riker and I aren't able to go to his home, Commander, would you send your team in again?" Eliana asked.

"You're implying my team missed something?" Riker asked.

"No. Yes. I don't know," Eliana said.

"Great, that cleared that right up," Riker replied with a playful tone.

She bit a fingernail then said, "Isn't it worth going over everything once more with a fine-toothed comb?"

"We haven't released the scene yet. Now is the time to do it," Skyler added. "What are we looking for?"

"That's just it, I'm not sure," Eliana said. "PHACE develops results based on appearance." She turned to look at the pickup. "But there's a component we're not considering. We're missing something."

"It can't hurt," Skyler said.

"We'll go through it again," Beckham assured her.

"One other thing." Eliana glanced at Riker, preparing for his refusal while hoping, with his team's support, he'd agree. "It's important for us to meet with Riker's parents and learn everything surrounding his birth."

Riker's eyes narrowed. "Not an option."

"I understand your hesitation, however, I disagree," Beckham argued. "Anything that helps us solve your case should be considered. Think it over, Riker. In the meantime, you two need to get on the road."

An engine's rumble interrupted the conversation.

"We'll keep you updated," Beckham promised, passing Riker a pistol. "Take this. I'll report your stolen duty weapon."

Riker expertly slid the gun in his waistband, keeping it from sight of the tow truck driver parking behind the F-150.

"There's an AR in the SUV as well," Skyler interjected.

"Thanks," Riker said.

"Eliana, keep brainstorming," Beckham encouraged. "We need fresh eyes on this case, and you might bring something we hadn't considered."

"I will." Now to convince Riker to talk to his parents.

"Ammo, come on, dude," Riker called.

The dogs barked, tackling one another playfully, ignoring their partners.

"Bosco," Skyler said.

The K-9 heeded his partner's command, gaining Ammo's attention. He halted then followed suit, looking for Riker and obeying the accompanying gesture. The intriguing partnerships had Eliana considering her own ways. Left alone, she was prone to wander, busy with her own activities, but with redirection, she conformed to God's lead.

Riker rewarded Ammo with the positive affirmation of a thorough back scratch. He understood Ammo's eagerness to obey and offered compassion when the dog failed.

She walked around the SUV and climbed into the passenger seat. *Lord, make me willing to obey You too. You know my heart, my desire to serve You and bring glory to You. When I forget who is in control, remind me, please.*

She snapped on her seat belt as Riker slid into the driver's seat. With a wave to Beckham and Skyler, they proceeded down the road.

A yawn caught her by surprise. "It's still morning, but it feels more like bedtime."

Riker grunted. "It has been a long forty-eight hours."

"So, remember our earlier conversation?" Eliana settled into the seat.

"Why do I feel like that's a loaded question?" A glimmer in his blue irises bolstered her courage.

"It is."

"Fire when ready."

"Before you say no, hear me out."

Riker grunted.

"As of right now, the only lead we have is the killer resembles you. We can't ignore the possibility he is a relative. Your folks may know something about your biological family."

He sighed. "Maybe."

Maybe was better than no.

SEVEN

They hadn't driven far before Riker's phone rang. He answered, activating the hands-free speakerphone. "Hey—"

"Where are you?" Beckham blurted.

"Highway 17 outside of Hooper. Why? What's wrong?"

"Turn around."

"What?"

"Captain Ferguson just called," Beckham replied as though that explained everything.

Had Omaha demanded his arrest? "Sir, we have seventy-two hours to produce—"

"Slow down and listen."

Eliana's wide eyes met his, and Riker swallowed hard.

"Moneyman's girlfriend stormed into Omaha's headquarters and demanded they investigate his death," Beckham elaborated.

"Say what?" Riker struggled to wrap his mind around the commander's comment. "This has to be a new record."

Eliana studied him, curiosity written in her expression.

"She might provide clues or help us fill in the blanks," Beckham added.

"I'm turning around," Riker replied, pulling over to the shoulder and preparing to make a U-turn.

"Hold on. You're not part of the investigation, remember? We'll handle it. I'm just keeping you up to date."

"I'm not asking to interrogate her, just to observe. I might pick up something you all miss," Riker said.

Beckham paused and finally spoke. "Okay, fair point. We're headed to the PD. I'll request they delay her interview until you arrive."

They disconnected. Waiting for a semi to pass before he made the turn, Riker commented, "This should be interesting."

"But what if her account makes things worse for you? Aren't we running into the burning building, so to speak?"

"The only way I'll get my life back, and both of us can stop looking over our shoulders, is to solve this case. In our situation, that means running toward the danger to get through it."

"I can't believe she's demanding justice," Eliana said.

"It has me reconsidering Moneyman's death. The GPS tracker and repeated attempts on our lives don't jibe. Why frame me for murder and then try to kill me? Moneyman was a big player in the D'Alfo Nites. One of the gang members might've betrayed him to rise in the power hierarchy."

"If that's true, why not wait and let their plan play out?" Eliana argued.

"Agreed. I think there are two separate enemies coming against us."

"You mean both with their own agendas?"

"Or are they working together? One wants to prevent you from testifying and demonstrating PHACE and its contribution to the last sting."

Eliana nodded. "Yeah, that makes sense." She twisted in her seat to face him. "Maybe I'm the target and you're collateral damage?"

"Except the killer tried to eliminate Ammo and me at your house."

"Or he shot at anyone who was searching? Nelson is a perfect example."

Riker mulled over the facts. "Hmm, good point. Okay, so why is someone framing me?"

"We find out the why and that'll tell us the who."

He'd witnessed an innocent person go to prison for a crime he didn't commit. Being a cop in prison was a death sentence in and of itself.

How many times had Riker prayed God would use him as He saw fit? Was he sincere? Or had he meant God would use him in a way Riker preferred? He'd heard many stories about people surrendering to whatever God used to draw them closer to Him. All of it sounded wonderful in a sermon, but real life and enduring suffering was a different story. *Lord, what if I'm not strong enough?* Would a prison sentence destroy Riker's faith in God?

"Why would someone want Moneyman dead?" Eliana asked, regaining his attention.

"He's got deep roots in the gang's finances and greed is always a top motivator for murder. Could be something as simple as the next person in line getting impatient about his promotion." Riker pondered the possibility. "Unless Moneyman is directly involved with the person wanting to frame me."

"Both had something to gain?"

"Or did Moneyman pose a threat of exposing the killer?" Even in the stress of working through the case, he appreciated Eliana discussing possibilities with him.

"Were the men PHACE identified on the last sting in line for promotion within the gang?" Eliana asked.

"No, that's the weird part. They were all lower-level thugs."

"Hmm."

They rode for several minutes in silence, passing only a couple of cars on their travels.

Riker's phone rang again, and he used the hands-free

speakerphone to answer, seeing it was Beckham again. "Sir."

"Eliana, you were right. Tiandra found a hair caught in the door hinge between the garage and mudroom at Riker's house. A *red* hair."

Both Riker and Moneyman were blond. The hair wasn't his.

"That's huge!" Eliana shot him a hopeful glance. "That proves someone else was there. Plus, red hair is unique and narrows down the possibilities. Can you get me the sample to run in PHACE?"

"Well, that's the bad news," Beckham said. "The hair is a partial, broken off from the original source."

Riker blinked, not understanding.

Eliana groaned. "And without a root, DNA testing won't provide a substantial result."

"Of course," Riker mumbled sarcastically.

"Regardless," Beckham interjected, "the find is helpful and places a third party at the scene, but it doesn't exclude Riker as the killer."

This time, Eliana appeared confused.

"Because the killer could've worn a wig while shooting Moneyman," Riker added, rubbing the back of his neck.

"On a positive note, the hair might also solidify you and the killer are not the same person. And there must be something in the coding that would make that distinction."

"That's what I'm hoping, Eliana," Beckham said. "We can talk more when you arrive. And, Riker, I'm keeping you informed for obvious reasons, but when you show up, don't overstep. You're still in the crosshairs here, and I don't want anything making your situation worse."

"Roger that." Riker disconnected. "One step forward, two steps back."

"No, this is definitely a positive," Eliana assured him. "Is it me or has it been too quiet?"

"I was thinking the same thing." He glanced in the rear-view mirror. "I just didn't want to speak the words."

They rounded a curve and the hairs on Riker's neck stood on end. He lifted his foot from the gas pedal, slowing.

"What's wrong?"

He didn't respond but listened, searching for anything suspicious.

Countryside spanned both sides of the road and a lone farmhouse stood in the distance. Tall overgrown grass swayed in the ditches. Fumes from the summer heat and gasoline danced above the black pavement. As they neared the deserted home, a shadow on the passenger side seemed to appear then vanish, catching Riker's attention. Had he imagined it?

"Riker!"

He jerked to look where Eliana pointed at a strip of spikes laid across the road. He slammed on the brakes and a bullet shattered the back window.

Riker swerved, driving the SUV off the shoulder before regaining control and preventing them from plunging into the ditch.

"Ammo, Eliana, down!"

The dog ducked, and Eliana slid lower in the seat.

Several more shots erupted, pelting the vehicle before a car squealed from the shadows of the old house, accelerating in the opposite direction.

"Are they gone?" Eliana slowly rose.

"Yes." Riker hit the brakes and called 9-1-1, reporting the incident and offering the limited information he remembered about the car.

Eliana twisted around in her seat, surveying the damage. She leaned over the console. "You're okay, sweetie."

Ammo popped his head through the divider.

"It's a good thing his kennel was steel and not opened to the back of the SUV."

Riker worked his jaw. "I recognized that car from the drive-by shooting in Omaha."

Eliana's eyes widened. "How'd they find us?"

He glanced at his cell phone and winced. "They've tapped into our phones."

"Please don't say I have to give up my phone."

"Only if you want to live."

"Ugh. I just paid it off!"

He quickly reported the incident to Beckham. "We're going to toss our phones. That's the only way they're tracking us."

"Understood. I'll have a set of burners ready for you."

"Roger that."

Riker disconnected and held out his hand. Eliana reluctantly placed her cell phone in his palm, and he exited the SUV, placing the devices beneath the front tire. He returned to the driver's seat and shifted into Drive, slowly rolling forward. Satisfied by the crunch that confirmed the destruction, they continued their trek.

"I cannot tell you how depressing that is," Eliana said.

"Maybe it'll help break your attachment to technology," he joked.

She groaned and settled back. "Since you brought it up, you carry a cell phone and use a laptop. You don't avoid technology."

"Can't deny that." Riker debated telling her the story then conceded, using the man's last name. "When I was a rookie, I worked on a case where the cops pinged this guy, Practor's cell phone and found the location of a kidnapped woman. They arrested him, and when the jury saw the evidence, it took them only a few hours to convict him. Practor was sentenced to twenty years."

"The device location proved he was the kidnapper."

"Except it didn't. He proclaimed his innocence, but it fell on deaf ears." Riker sighed. "Technological advancements are a great thing. But between television and movies depicting forensic work in a speeded format, the jury has unrealistic expectations."

"The CSI effect," Eliana clarified.

"Yes, they see something like a cell phone pinging and *poof*, the rest falls into place. But that wasn't the end of the case. The kidnappers had stolen Practor's phone and used it in the kidnapping."

Eliana gasped. "No."

"Yep, and it took years for him to be exonerated from the crime. By then, he'd lost his family, his home and his job. Not to mention the stigma the media stained him with. Even though he was innocent, the public deemed him guilty."

"That's terrible. No wonder you're adamant about not using technology in investigations."

"I just don't want it to be the deciding factor. Everything in this case makes me look guilty. But, Eliana, I didn't kill Moneyman."

"I believe you."

"I appreciate your vote of confidence," Riker said.

She smiled.

"What if the killer used Moneyman then had to eliminate him?"

"You've got my full attention," Eliana replied.

"He's the one in charge of the money, thus the nickname. If he had an abundance of cash on him at the time of the murder, the killer could've taken the money and run. He gets the perfect escape by putting the blame on me and disappearing to live free without suspicion."

"Makes sense to me," Eliana agreed. "And the gang would think you have the money in your possession, which means they'll keep hunting you."

"Right."

They settled into a comfortable silence, but Riker's curiosity overrode his common sense. He had the opportunity to talk to Eliana, and he wouldn't waste it. "I have a question for you."

"Should I be afraid?" she quipped.

Their banter was easy and light. And he was about to ruin it. "No. Please tell me why you left school without saying goodbye."

Her expression tightened. "It's complicated." She turned away, immediately shifting the atmosphere.

Eliana stared out the window, contemplating how much to reveal. The answer to Riker's question was more complex than he understood.

"Your silence is only building the suspense." Though Riker's comment held a playfulness, she refused to face him.

"Let's leave the past behind us. A lot has happened since then and we have bigger issues to deal with."

After several silent beats, he said, "Correct."

She'd offended him, but rehashing her past offered nothing positive. What would he think of her if he learned the truth about her con man father? She was also using Riker's team to get an endorsement for PHACE to help propel her search for her brother's killer. She should disclose that to Riker, yet she remained silent. She hated the quiet dissension that hung between them but telling Riker about either wasn't an option.

At the point of bursting from the dead air, Eliana reengaged him by pondering theories and working the clues aloud. By the time Riker pulled up to the Omaha PD headquarters office, their conversation returned to a cordial albeit rigid discussion.

Eliana reached for the door handle, glancing at Riker, who was fixated on something beyond her. She turned, following his gaze. An officer assisted a handcuffed man from the back of a patrol car in front of them.

"He hardly looks like a criminal, huh?" Riker spoke the

YOU pick your books –
WE pay for everything.
You get up to FOUR New Books and TWOMystery Gifts...absolutely FREE!

Dear Reader,

I am writing to announce the launch of a huge **FREE BOOK GIVEAWAY**... and to let you know that YOU are entitled to choose up to FOUR fantastic books that WE pay for.

Try **Love Inspired® Romance Larger-Print** books and fall in love with inspirational romances that take you on an uplifting journey of faith, forgiveness and hope.

Try **Love Inspired® Suspense Larger-Print** books where courage and optimism unite in stories of faith and love in the face of danger.

Or TRY BOTH!

In return, we ask just one favor: Would you please participate in our brief Reader Survey? We'd love to hear from you.

This FREE BOOKS GIVEAWAY means that your introductory shipment is completely free, <u>even the shipping</u>! If you decide to continue, you can look forward to curated monthly shipments of brand-new books from your selected series, always at a discount off the cover price! <u>Plus you can cancel any time</u>. Who could pass up a deal like that?

Sincerely,

Pam Powers

Pam Powers
For Harlequin Reader Service

Complete the survey below and return it today to receive up to 4 FREE BOOKS and FREE GIFTS guaranteed!

FREE BOOKS GIVEAWAY
Reader Survey

1

Do you prefer books which reflect Christian values?

◯ YES   ◯ NO

2

Do you share your favorite books with friends?

◯ YES   ◯ NO

3

Do you often choose to read instead of watching TV?

◯ YES   ◯ NO

YES! Please send me my Free Rewards, consisting of **2 Free Books from each series I select** and **Free Mystery Gifts**. I understand that I am under no obligation to buy anything, no purchase necessary see terms and conditions for details.

❏ **Love Inspired® Romance Larger-Print** (122/322 IDL GRP7)
❏ **Love Inspired® Suspense Larger-Print** (107/307 IDL GRP7)
❏ **Try Both** (122/322 & 107/307 IDL GRQK)

FIRST NAME	LAST NAME

ADDRESS

APT.#	CITY

STATE/PROV.	ZIP/POSTAL CODE

EMAIL ❏ Please check this box if you would like to receive newsletters and promotional emails from Harlequin Enterprises ULC and its affiliates. You can unsubscribe anytime.

LI/LIS-122-FBG22_LI/LIS-122-FBGVR

HARLEQUIN® Reader Service — Terms and Conditions:

BUSINESS REPLY MAIL
FIRST-CLASS MAIL   PERMIT NO. 717   BUFFALO, NY

POSTAGE WILL BE PAID BY ADDRESSEE

HARLEQUIN READER SERVICE
PO BOX 1341
BUFFALO NY 14240-8571

NO POSTAGE
NECESSARY
IF MAILED
IN THE
UNITED STATES

◀ If offer card is missing write to: Harlequin Reader Service, P.O. Box 1341, Buffalo, NY 14240-8531 or visit www.ReaderService.com ◀

question so softly she wondered if he was thinking aloud. "What was he accused of doing?" He shut off the engine and reached for the door handle. "Wonder if I'll be returning to this place in handcuffs too?"

Sympathy for Riker enveloped her and for the first time, she understood he truly feared going to prison. They piled out of the SUV and she waited as Riker leashed Ammo.

In a silent march, they trudged to the front doors. Though she had no reason to feel self-conscious, the busy office intimidated her, and she imagined how it impacted Riker. Officers and civilians scurried from phones to offices, and Eliana couldn't shake the feeling they were being scrutinized. She glanced over her shoulder, catching the eye of a younger cop, who met her gaze. He leaned against a cubical wall, conversing with an attractive woman seated at a desk. Eliana offered a small smile, but neither returned the gesture. She averted her eyes and hurried to catch up to Riker, who remained stoic, ignoring or unaware of the situation.

They rounded a corner into a hallway, where closed doors lined both sides. Without hesitation, Riker aimed for the one ajar at the far end. He rapped twice below a metal sign that read Observation Room #2, and they entered.

Soft light glowed where Commander Walsh and Captain Ferguson occupied the cramped space. Beckham waved them inside and Riker shifted, allowing Eliana to go ahead of him before closing the door. The group stood in front of a large window that viewed Interrogation Room #2.

"Captain Ferguson offered for us to watch from here." Eliana cued into Beckham's subtle reminder that Omaha PD had no obligation to include them in any part of the investigation.

Riker and Ammo pressed against the furthest end of the wall and Riker lifted his hand, signaling the dog. He sat and softly panted.

Inside the adjoining room, a woman sat opposite Officer Marvin. Neither spoke, and Eliana wondered how long they'd been that way. The pretty twentysomething wore her black hair spiked up randomly over her head in a fashionista style, and her heavy eye makeup made her dark eyes seem larger. She wore jean shorts and a short-sleeved T-shirt with swirls of pink and blue on the white cotton fabric. She tapped her long fingernails in a rhythm on the metal tabletop.

Graham entered the room and slid into the chair beside Officer Marvin. "Good afternoon. I'm Graham Kenyon with the DEA."

"Hey," the woman replied dully.

"This is two-way glass, and the room is sound-proofed," Riker whispered to Eliana. "They cannot hear or see us."

She nodded, eyes fixed on the scene playing before her like those she'd witnessed in crime television shows.

"I apologize for the delay in my arrival. Thank you for being kind enough to wait for me, Miss York," Graham said.

"Noella," she corrected. "I've already told this guy everything."

"I apologize for the inconvenience, but would you repeat it to me? We don't want anything lost in translation." Graham flashed a winning smile.

She grunted and slid back in the chair, crossing her arms over her chest. "You found Orion's body at that Dundee house. Why ain't you arrested the owner yet?"

Officer Marvin leaned closer. "We'd like to."

Riker stiffened beside Eliana. "I'm sure *we* would," he mumbled.

From her peripheral, she caught Beckham's disapproving frown. Had he overheard Riker or was he annoyed by Marvin's response? The dynamics of the relationship between law enforcement intrigued her and dislodged her assumption they were all a big brotherhood dutifully bound to back one another.

"We need more evidence," Graham told her. "I understand you have something that will help us find out what happened to Moneyman."

She unfolded her arms and leaned forward. "*Orion.* That was his name," she snapped, pointing a daggered nail. "He was a human being with a real name and a real life."

"Agreed, but he was also a prominent fixture in the D'Alfo Nites," Graham argued.

She snorted in a not very ladylike way. "It's easy to judge us when you didn't grow up how we did. You only see what's printed on that paper about Orion. But you didn't know him, and you weren't surviving the streets before you were outta diapers either."

Eliana monitored Riker's reaction to the woman's response. Crime was never justifiable, but she understood being an unwilling participant in difficult circumstances. Compassion swelled Eliana's heart. Noella may have fallen in love with the wrong guy. If he'd protected her from the criminals on the streets, Orion was her hero.

"That's true," Graham conceded. "We're not here to judge. That's far above both our pay grades. We want to solve Orion's murder."

Noella resumed her defensive posture, arms crossed at her chest. "Then why haven't you arrested the house owner?"

"Unfortunately, location alone doesn't prove who killed Orion," Graham replied. "However, if you are able to provide evidence leading to Orion's killer, that might give us the go-ahead we need."

Eliana spun to look at Riker and he shrugged. "He needs to win her over."

"Oh," she replied.

"Why would Orion be at that house? Was he acquainted

with the owner?" Marvin passed a picture of Riker to the woman.

Eliana's defenses rose. "He's supposed to be on Riker's side."

"He's on the side of truth," Captain Ferguson replied softly.

"Yeah," the woman said, regaining their attention. She stabbed a pointed nail at the picture. "That's Blaze."

Graham flicked a glance briefly at the window, but the move was almost imperceptible. "Blaze?"

"That's him, taken just before he dyed his hair that stupid color," Noella replied, grabbing her cell phone from the table. She swiped a clawed finger at the screen before setting it before the officers to view.

Marvin reached for it first, studied the picture with a smile, then spun the device around to face Graham.

His movements were slow and calculated as he lifted the bedazzled phone. "This is Blaze?"

"Yep. That was just two months ago at a party." She leaned forward, her tone dripping with accusation. "Word is that house belongs to a cop. Figures, he played dirty and conned my man, then killed him."

"How did Blaze con Orion?" Graham probed.

She hesitated then said, "Pretending to be his friend and all." She clammed up as though realizing she might've said too much.

"May I borrow this?" Graham pushed away from the table, Noella's phone in hand.

"Just bring it right back," she snapped.

Graham hurried out and entered the observation room. "You'll want to see this."

Eliana, Riker and the commanders huddled around him, and Riker took the phone, displaying it for the others to see. The picture showed a man holding a blue plastic cup, grinning wide, and surrounded by Noella York and Orion Potts.

"He totally resembles you," Eliana said, surveying the man's features. Bone structure and stature appeared almost identical to Riker, except for the badly dyed red hair. "I had a friend who used cheap hair dye. Turned her hair that color too."

"Like a clown wig," Graham said.

"Definitely not his natural color. If we had a sample of Blaze's hair, we could compare it to the one found in Riker's house," she pondered aloud. "He must've tried dying his mustache, too, though the color is a little more believable." She glanced at Riker. His dark blond hair held no red highlights at all. Changing hair color was easy, but there was no disputing Blaze was Riker's mirror image.

"That's not me," Riker contested softly, eyes fixed on the phone.

But if a picture was worth a thousand words, this one was worth a twenty-to-life prison sentence.

EIGHT

Eliana's mind raced with possibilities.

"Dude, Noella confirmed they took this picture two months ago." Graham pointed to the time stamp on the photo.

Curiosity at the implication of that information had Eliana's gaze bouncing between the men. "We were working the case in Des Moines!" Riker exclaimed.

"Precisely!" Graham gave an emphatic nod.

"But it doesn't help us figure out Blaze's real identity," Captain Ferguson countered.

"No, but it provides reasonable plausibility that whoever Blaze is, he's got it in for Riker," Beckham said. "Good work, Graham. Let's see what else Noella offers."

"On it." Graham scurried out and returned to the room where Noella sat tapping her fingernails on the table.

They both glanced up at his approach and Eliana noticed Marvin wore skepticism like his badge. "We have confirmation of an inside job."

"Can't say for sure yet, but certainly shifts the focus," Graham replied.

Eliana grinned.

Graham continued. "Noella, you and Orion are in this picture with Blaze. Are you certain about when it was taken?"

Eliana glanced at Riker. The date stamp was an automated feature. Why was Graham pressing? She also noted he didn't share the alibi information with Marvin, countering his accusation that Riker was guilty. She suspected his tactics were an intentional move to keep Noella believing they were on her side and swallowing her story.

Graham passed Noella her phone and she nodded emphatically. "That was Orion's big birthday bash. The whole family was there."

"You mean the Nites?" Graham asked.

She narrowed her eyes and leaned forward. "That *is* our family."

"I get it," Graham replied. "Why would Blaze kill Orion, especially if they were friends?"

Noella crossed her arms over her chest. "When I saw the news, I did a little digging."

"Great." Marvin's comment dripped with sarcasm. "Everyone thinks they are expert investigators with the internet these days."

She pinned him with a glower. "Except I'm sitting here handing you the killer while you're doing nothing."

He lifted a hand in surrender and Eliana forced away a smile. *Go, Noella.*

"Anyway." She reverted her attention to Graham. "The cop's house where Orion was killed, I looked it up and found the owner's name. And what do you know? Riker Kastell is Blaze. Must've been working undercover—the sneak—except he probably figured he'd just take the money and run. After he killed my man."

"Wow, we should hire you for our intelligence unit," Graham said.

Eliana heard no condemnation in his tone. "Actually, she'd probably be a great resource if you could trust her," she whispered to Riker.

He frowned. "The best CIs are."

"Blaze called Orion the night—" Noella's voice cracked and she paused, pressing a hand against her painted lips.

"Take your time," Graham said.

"Thing is, we trusted him." Noella shook her head.

Eliana couldn't tear her gaze from the interrogation. If Noella had found the information on Riker, that meant the press would do the same.

"Are you certain that was the same night Orion went missing? The same night he was shot?" Marvin pressed.

"Yes." She nodded emphatically. "Orion got a call from Blaze saying he had something big, but he insisted Orion come alone."

"Do you normally accompany Orion on visits with Blaze?" Graham queried.

"Sometimes, but not on business meetings."

"Business?" Marvin sneered. "Or drug deals?"

Noella glared at him. "Of course, you'd go there."

"Well, it's hard not to since I have this." Marvin opened a file folder on the table and pointed to the papers. "Lincoln PD recently arrested you for possession."

"The drugs weren't mine, and they dismissed the charges," Noella countered.

Riker snorted. "Right."

Eliana glanced up at him.

"Most of them," Marvin added.

"Look, you want my help or not?" Noella snapped.

Eliana's gaze bounced between the scene unfolding in front of her and the reaction of Riker, Captain Ferguson, and Beckham standing beside her.

"Yes, we do, Noella," Graham said, regaining control over the conversation. "Did you hear from Orion once he left to meet Blaze?"

"No." She glanced down at the table. "Said he'd be back in an hour and never came home. That was the last I saw of him."

"You've taken an enormous risk coming here," Graham said. "Are the Nites aware you're talking to us?"

"No." She lifted her chin defiantly and fixed her gaze on Marvin.

"Do you fear for your safety?" Graham asked.

She turned to face him, her expression softening. "You couldn't protect me if you wanted to. You cops have no clue."

"If your information leads to the arrest of Orion's killer, we'll provide a protection detail for you," Graham insisted.

"For how long? Forever?" She rolled her eyes, resuming her tough exterior. "Do you know how many funerals I go to in a year? Please."

"Some family the Nites are," Marvin commented sarcastically.

"Are they talking retribution?" Graham asked.

She shrugged. "You judge Orion as a criminal, but he was different with me. I loved him. He didn't deserve what happened to him."

"Why would Blaze want to kill him?" Graham asked, compassion in his tone. "You said they were friends."

Noella seemed to consider the question before responding. "I figure Orion made Blaze as a cop and threatened to tell the Nites."

"Do you have evidence to support that?" Graham asked.

"No, but it makes sense." Noella tapped her phone. "He pulled one over on us. Probably thought he could play both worlds. Take advantage."

Eliana considered Noella's reasoning and agreed she wasn't totally off base. "Did you work undercover?" she whispered to Riker.

He responded with a quick shake of his head.

Beckham's phone rang. "Excuse me." He stepped out of the room.

Riker placed a hand on the small of Eliana's back when it was clear the interrogation was over. "Let's go."

They stepped into the hallway just as Beckham exited an office on the opposite side and waved them over. Graham walked out of the interview room and joined them. The group assembled around the metal table and slid into the chairs. Ammo sat beside Riker.

Beckham handed Riker two burner cell phones. "Use these for now. We'll work on getting your phones replaced when this is over."

"Thanks." Riker pocketed one and passed the other to Eliana.

"That phone call was about Nelson," Beckham stated, gaining the group's full attention. "The doctors removed the bullets that tore through his trapezius muscle. They came within millimeters of hitting his heart. He's in recovery and should progress well."

Riker's throat tightened and relief nearly buckled his knees. *Thank You, Lord.* "That's great news."

Eliana's eyes welled with tears. "I'm glad he's going to be okay."

"Me too." Riker gave another silent prayer of thanks. With the news of Nelson's condition, his focus returned entirely on finding this criminal and making sure he never saw life outside of prison walls.

"The department is providing round-the-clock security for Nelson and his family," Beckham added.

"We'll make sure he's covered," Graham assured them.

"Please keep me updated should anything change," Riker said.

"Meet with the Omaha PD gang unit, Graham, and see if they have any information on this Blaze character," Beckham ordered.

Graham nodded. "On it."

"With all due respect, Noella is accusing Riker of posing as Blaze and claiming he killed Moneyman," Eliana said. "Doesn't that seem a little too convenient?"

"I'm with her," Graham affirmed.

"We finally have a viable suspect—this Blaze fellow. Although—" Riker rubbed the day's growth on his chin "—did you notice the way she kept looking at Marvin?"

Confused, Eliana asked, "You mean the way she glared at him? There's no love between them."

"It was subtle, but I picked up on the nuance too," Graham said.

"Think he coerced her?" Riker asked.

"Guys, we need to be careful here," Beckham warned.

"Just thinking out loud," Graham mused. "It's possible, and she did come in with him. He could've talked to her beforehand. Or suggested a plea deal of some sort. Noella's got a criminal history. Nothing major but enough that working off some charges might be beneficial, especially for a mother-to-be."

"What?" Riker's eyes widened.

"How did you figure that out?" Eliana questioned.

"It was in her photos. A Coming Soon announcement," Graham said with a slight grin. "My cousin did one of those."

"Good work," Beckham commended. "If Blaze is the shooter, it doesn't explain the picture he put in Moneyman's pocket of Riker and his family. We need that connection."

"Forensic genealogy has proved useful in solving big cases. I think we could use it here," Eliana persisted.

"Riker?" Beckham asked.

"Fine." He exhaled a long sigh. "After all the death attempts on our lives, it might be beneficial to get out of Nebraska for a while, and see my folks."

"Agreed," Beckham said.

"We'll keep you updated," Graham assured them, getting to his feet. "I'll reach out to my gang unit contact." He opened the door and nearly collided with Marvin, blocking the doorway.

Had he been eavesdropping?

"What can we do for you?" Beckham asked the officer.

"Why is he here?" Marvin entered, glare fixed on Riker.

"We have team business to conduct," Beckham answered, though Eliana was certain he had no obligation to explain.

Marvin harrumphed. "Makes my job easier. I've got an eyewitness who says you're the killer. That gives me enough to arrest you."

"Actually," Beckham argued, "Noella York confirmed Blaze and Riker are not one and the same person."

Marvin blinked and stood taller. "She places Riker, aka Blaze, with Moneyman on the night of his murder."

Eliana watched the exchange. Was Marvin unaware they'd been watching through the two-way window?

"Our team worked a case out of state on the date of the party," Beckham said. "There's no way Riker could be in two places at the same time."

Marvin's face burned a bright crimson and his eyes seemed to bulge from his head. "We'll see about that. Stick close, Marshal." He stormed out, shutting the door harder than necessary behind him.

Riker shook his head. "What's his problem?"

"Focus on the end goal." Beckham moved to the door. "Check in every couple of hours and use the code to text your location. The burners don't have GPS but keep them powered off unless they're in use."

"Roger that." Riker paused. "One other thing. In the latest attack, the shooter blasted out the back window of Skyler's SUV."

Beckham groaned. "I'm running out of vehicles to give you."

Riker shrugged. "I'd prefer to use my personal truck."

"I don't know."

With his most convincing smile, Riker said, "At least if something happens to it, you won't be stuck explaining how I ruined any more team vehicles."

Eliana stifled a giggle.

Beckham chuckled. "Fine. Leave Skyler's ride at your house. We'll pick it up and get it repaired."

"Thanks."

"Let's get out of here." Riker stood and led Eliana out of the office, passing officers and personnel without comment.

Each wore expressions that spanned everything from curiosity and condemnation to sympathy. When they reached the front steps, he inhaled the fresh air and hastened away from the building.

Graham hurried behind them. "Marvin is not a happy guy."

Riker grunted. "He's made that clear. I want to scream 'It's not me!'"

"The truth will come out. Hang in there."

"Graham, we might need your help in a little while," Eliana said.

Riker flicked a glance at her. "For what?"

"Ammo needs a break." She gave a jerk of her chin toward a grassy area away from the precinct doors.

Riker caught her hint, and they crossed the parking lot, but Ammo moved toward the SUV. "He thinks we're leaving." Riker tugged on the leash. "Come on, over here." The dog ignored him, straining to reach the vehicle.

"He didn't hear you," Eliana said.

Riker halted and his K-9 turned to face him. "Go." He gestured at the grass, eliciting a whine from Ammo before he complied.

Once they reached some distance out of hearing of any passersby, Riker said, "Okay, give me something to hang on to."

"Noella had posted the picture on a popular social media site…" Eliana began. "Would you send us a screenshot?"

"Sure," Graham said, skepticism in his tone. "I'd better head inside and find out what Beckham wants to do next. Have faith, Riker." He slapped his friend on the back and jogged to the headquarters' doors.

"How is social media going to help me?" Riker asked, leading the way to Skyler's SUV.

"Let's get away from here before we talk more," Eliana suggested.

They climbed in the vehicle, Ammo jumping in with them.

Once they were on the road again, Eliana continued. "People will tag others in their social media posts. We'll use that facial recognition to identify Blaze."

"That's brilliant."

She beamed under his approval. "One step at a time. I've been experimenting with an additional feature in PHACE, incorporating social media factors. Since we don't have access to certified databases."

Riker winced. "Sorry about my earlier snide comment."

"It's all good. I really want to start on this. Would it be possible to postpone going to the cabin and instead find someplace where I can work?"

"Sure, but not here."

Riker drove east, pulling into the first town outside of Omaha. He parked in front of a single-story brick building with a badly painted sign that read Library. Barely able to contain his eagerness, he spoke with the man behind the desk and requested a study room where they could work privately.

Once settled, Riker paced with anticipation while Eliana typed away on her laptop. Riker passed her the cell phone with the image Graham provided. She launched a new search window and scoured through sites. Eliana clicked so quickly between each one, Riker gave up trying to follow along.

"Social media stalking," she explained.

He chuckled. "I see that."

She paused and zoomed in on one site. "Found him."

Riker leaned over her shoulder.

"He was active here until a few months ago. That's ancient history in the computer world, but if I can drill down and find his name…" Her voice trailed off as she resumed typing and scrolling through the screen.

Riker stood and continued pacing. Ammo watched him, ears alert. "We've worked the Nites nonstop for over a year. I've never heard of Blaze."

"But they have thousands of members, right?"

"Yes. All over the country."

"Aha," she announced.

Riker turned and dropped into the chair beside her. The screen showed a post over three years old. Even with the man's full beard and long hair concealing much of his facial features, there was no denying the resemblance.

"Enough of the characteristic points match PHACE, which explains the composite sketch," Eliana said, nibbling on a fingernail. "We need access to the DMV database."

An idea bloomed and Riker reached for the computer. "May I?"

Eliana nodded, turning the screen to him. Riker opened a new window and typed the link for the Nebraska Criminal Justice Information System. He logged in, only to receive an error message. Frustrated, he pushed away from the table. "They've locked me out." His phone rang and he answered.

"Riker, what have I told you about getting online and poking around the investigation?" Beckham barked. "You're making it harder for me to do my job."

Eliana watched with interest, and Riker winced. "The system pinged me."

"What're you thinking? You can't make that rookie-foolish move without me knowing."

"You'll change your mind when we tell you what Eliana found."

"I'm listening," Beckham grumbled.

"Eliana located Blaze's social media account. Anyone would have access," Riker pointed out, more determined than ever to get answers to clear his name.

"And?"

"If we continue drilling down, we might find more information. Like his real name."

"Negative."

"We could use the DMV pictures and run facial recognition there," Riker argued.

"Riker, let us do this. Graham is working with the gang unit," Beckham reminded him. "We'll keep you updated. Get the info from your parents about your biological family."

"Roger that." Riker disconnected. "I have an idea, but I'll probably get myself into trouble."

She held up her hand. "Nope. Sounds like we already did that. We should stop. I don't want you to do anything that might jeopardize your case." She closed the laptop. "We've given your team information they can use to continue investigating."

"Maybe you're right. I don't want to give Marvin any excuse to arrest me. The guy probably won't sleep until he does."

They loaded their stuff, walked out to the SUV and climbed inside. Ammo sat on the ground at the back of the vehicle again. "Ammo. Come."

The K-9 whined and got to his feet, obediently moving to Riker's side.

Once they were on the road, Eliana asked, "Could we grab some lunch?"

Ammo poked his head through the separator and whined his agreement.

"Sure," Riker chuckled. "Any place in particular?"

"Probably something portable," Eliana replied.

He glanced at the dashboard clock. A stop might not be a bad idea. "Let's swap vehicles first."

"Sounds good."

Riker considered the condition of Skyler's SUV. The blown-out back window made the SUV an easy target for thieves. He'd need to put her vehicle in the garage. Fortunately, it was no longer a crime scene, so he wouldn't be violating any rules by being there.

When they completed the brief commute to his home, he parked on the street and left the engine running. "Give me a sec." He hopped out of the SUV and jogged up the driveway.

The comfort of familiarity warred with the uncertain sadness of when he'd come home for good. He typed in the code for the garage door, activating its release. A groan accompanied the rising door as though it understood the weight Riker bore. He ducked inside and surveyed the area.

Black fingerprint powder covered the walls, doors and cabinets. Would he have to repaint everything? He'd spent years painstakingly restoring the property. His whole life had become a disaster.

He sighed and slid behind the wheel of his pickup, then shifted into Reverse and backed out of the garage. Parking the truck in front of the house, he returned to the SUV and pulled the vehicle into the garage.

"Are you okay?" Eliana asked, compassion in her emerald irises.

"Not really." He exited the SUV and released Ammo to his familiar lawn. "I'll let him wander around while we work."

"He's probably glad to be home."

At least temporarily.

They transferred their possessions from the SUV into the truck without speaking. When they'd finished, Riker turned, searching for Ammo. "Where did he go?"

Eliana scanned the property. "He was here a second ago."

"Ammo." Riker walked the yard, Eliana just behind him.

Dark brindle fur scurried at the far side of his backyard. Ammo sniffed the lawn with meticulous precision.

"Hey, buddy, it's time to leave again." He didn't respond, so Riker shifted into Ammo's line of vision and repeated the command. Sadness filled the dog's soulful eyes as he gazed up. Tenderness for his partner filled Riker's heart and he knelt, stroking Ammo's fur. "I want to come home too. Soon, buddy—"

An explosion rocked the ground, thrusting Riker off balance. He teetered to the side and turned to see smoke pluming from the front of the house.

"Eliana!" His ears rang. He searched the yard, finding her facedown in the grass several feet away, Ammo licking at her cheek. Riker pushed to his feet and hurried to them. "Eliana."

She groaned and pushed herself up. Riker helped her sit, sending silent prayers of thanks that she was alive. "Are you okay?"

"I think so. What happened?"

"I'm not sure, but we need to get out of here."

"Shouldn't we wait for the police and firefighters?"

"No." Riker visually searched for any danger. "We must get somewhere safe. We're too exposed."

Together they rushed around the house, where Skyler's SUV smoldered, the whole back end wide open as though someone had pried it apart with a giant can opener. Debris covered his yard and driveway. Only the front of the garage had sustained minor damage. His personal vehicle had gone unharmed. Nothing compared to the SUV. *Skyler will strangle me.* He ran a hand over his neck.

They loaded into his truck and hurried out of the neighborhood.

"Call Beckham and put it on speakerphone."

Eliana did as he asked, and his commander answered on the first ring.

"Boss, you'll never believe this." Riker provided a synopsis of the events. "Somehow make the killer believe he succeeded, at least for a little while, to give Eliana and me a chance to get as far away as possible."

"Turn off the phone and check in within an hour from wherever you are," Beckham said.

"Will do."

Eliana turned off the device. "If Ammo hadn't wandered off, we'd be dead."

"I know." He glanced at her, and the look in her eyes conveyed she understood completely. Ammo had saved their lives.

"How did the killer get a bomb into the SUV and detonate it?"

"Probably using a cell phone timer." Riker sighed. "Getting it into the SUV was my fault."

"How so?"

"Do you remember the number of times Ammo returned to sit at the rear of the SUV?"

Eliana tilted her head. "Yeah, that was strange."

"No, it was me not paying attention. He's an explosion detection dog. I should've recognized his signal, but I was too busy in my own brain. He tried to tell us." Regret and anger at himself had Riker wanting to punch something.

Ever intuitive, Ammo poked his head over the headrest.

"I am sorry, dude." Riker reached up with one hand and stroked the dog's velvety ears.

"But when did the killer put a bomb into the SUV? We were at the police station and the library," Eliana asked.

"He's following or tracking us somehow."

"How? We've tossed our phones and traded vehicles."

"Never underestimate the determination of someone who wants you dead," Riker replied. "And we have two villains after us."

Eliana groaned. "This has to end sometime."

"It will after we expose them for who they are. Sometimes survival is about fighting back on the offensive, not just the defensive."

NINE

Riker drove thirty minutes before he pulled through a fast-food lane and placed their orders, including a plain burger for Ammo. Once they'd paid for their food, he continued toward Lake Conner. He found the optimal place, drove down the small lane and parked beneath a canopy of trees near the water.

"Will this work?"

Eliana smiled. "It's perfect."

Keeping one eye on Ammo and the other scanning for any potential dangers, Riker tucked the Glock that Beckham had loaned him into his waistband. With food in hand, they made their way to the table. Ammo pranced in the remnants of grass that intermingled with weeds threatening to overtake it.

Trees heavily laden with leaves provided shade overhead, and Eliana set their lunch on an old picnic table pockmarked by time chipping away at the red paint. A soft breeze fluttered her hair, and the sun accentuated the gold flecks in her eyes. She smiled, drawing attention to her full lips.

Why did she have to be so beautiful?

In an unfamiliar quandary, Riker realized he didn't want their time together to end. Still, the unrelenting threats on their lives took a toll on all of them. He needed to reside in the resentment he'd grown accustomed to, cloaked beneath disdain for Eliana and her stupid computer program.

If only his heart would comply.

The way she awakened his senses made him dizzy with feelings he'd long ago tucked away. It had been easy to avoid her in the office, maintaining a distance and allowing his teammates to run interference between them. Alone with Eliana, he struggled to keep the disinterested attitude he'd worked so hard to portray. When he stopped to admire the woman before him, she was the only thing he saw.

"I don't think fried grease and unhealthy calories ever tasted so good." Eliana withdrew a few fries, stuffing them into her mouth, and passed him a burger.

Riker nodded, shoving away his contemplations, and inhaled the salty delight. "Agreed."

"At least the weather is cooperating." Eliana handed him a paper-wrapped straw, brushing his fingers with hers.

Her soft touch, like an electric shock, had him jerking back. He shoved the straw through the lid, hoping she hadn't noticed. Averting his eyes, he sipped the soda and relished the caffeinated cola. "Guess they didn't get hit with that monsoon Fremont did last night." He gestured to the dry ground beneath the table.

Ammo returned from his short exploration activities and sat beside Riker, panting softly.

"Welcome back." Riker broke apart the plain hamburger and placed it before Ammo on the paper wrapping. "Have at it."

In three bites, Ammo inhaled the food then licked his chops.

Eliana snickered. "He was hungry too."

Riker bit into the triple cheeseburger, savoring the deliciousness that consumed his senses. "I rarely eat fast food, so this is a treat."

"Me too." She sipped on her chocolate milkshake. "Some

things go together well, you know? Like burgers, fries and milkshakes."

Like us. The unbidden thought reminded Riker of their first date. Despite his heart's warning not to go there, he said, "I remember. I'd never seen a girl eat a triple cheeseburger before you."

She tilted her head as though jarring the memory loose, then laughed. "Are you talking about the church group movie night? I don't think that qualifies as a first date for the record."

He nodded, munching on a French fry. "It does too. We agreed chaperoned or group dates were the safe way to keep from falling into temptation."

"You're right. I totally forgot about that." She grinned wide and covered her mouth. "When I get nervous, I eat. That night, I was ravenous." Eliana sipped the milkshake again.

"I never would've thought that. You always seemed so confident."

"If only." She glanced down and the sun's rays highlighted her auburn hair. "I figured if I kept eating, I wouldn't say anything stupid." Eliana swirled a fry in ketchup.

"I'll try that technique."

"I must admit, meeting your parents is intimidating. Have you called them to let them know we're coming?"

Several silent beats passed and Riker turned to look at the lake. She didn't understand. He dreaded pressing his parents for information about his adoption. Would it hurt them?

"Riker?"

"No." He twisted around and stuffed a bite into his mouth, stalling under Eliana's questioning gaze. After swallowing, he said, "They'll be fine. Mom loves surprises."

Probably not the one he was about to unleash on her.

Riker's burner phone rang, mercifully interrupting the

uncomfortable discussion, and he placed it on speaker-phone. "Graham, go ahead, we're both listening."

"Same here with the team," Graham confirmed. "Those gang unit guys are too cool."

Riker chuckled. "Beyond making new friends, did you find anything?"

"Oh, yeah. For starters, Blaze is Todd Billings," Graham said.

Riker rolled the name around in his mind. "Never heard of him."

"That's because he's an under-the-radar type of guy who manages to squeeze through the system," Tiandra explained. "He's a frequent flyer."

"Yeah," Skyler intoned, "he's familiar with metal brace-lets."

Eliana quirked a brow.

"A repeat offender. He has an arrest record," Riker whispered.

"Oh," she replied.

"His rap sheet shows a few arrests, petty crimes mostly," Skyler related. "Affiliation with the Nites, but those charges were dismissed."

Riker sighed. "No convictions?"

"What's that mean?" Eliana asked.

"Todd Billings has no DNA on file," Riker explained.

"Which means there's no comparable sample," Eliana replied.

Riker spoke into the phone. "Bring him in for questioning."

"Already working on that, but my contact at the gang unit says he's eluded them on other cases they're working," Graham said. "Todd's been off the grid for a while."

Eliana leaned closer. "That's gotta say something."

"Or it means Todd's dead," Graham replied.

"I don't understand," Eliana said.

"When a gang member goes missing for an extended period, the first assumption is they're dead," Riker clarified. "Except in this case, Todd is looking good for Moneyman's death."

"Graham forwarded Todd's DMV picture to Eliana's email," Beckham said.

"Dude, wait until you see it." Graham's excitement oozed through the line.

"Okay now it's my turn to die of suspense. I'll grab my computer." Eliana jumped to her feet and hurried to the truck, returning with the laptop. "Logging in now."

"We need to figure out why Todd has it out for you," Tiandra said.

"Pulling up the picture." Eliana gasped and turned the screen to face him.

Riker's doppelganger stared back at him. "I don't know Todd Billings."

"He could pass for your twin," Eliana exclaimed.

"We have different dates of birth," Riker argued, unsure why he was refuting the possibility. "There's no way we're twins."

"Actually, your DOBs are only off by a week. Same year," Graham noted.

"Twins aren't born a week apart," Riker challenged.

"When I was in nursing school, we learned about a procedure called delayed-interval delivery," Tiandra said.

"You went to nursing school?" Graham asked.

"Focus," Riker snapped. "What's the delayed thing you were talking about?"

"The doctor delivers one twin, while the other remains in vitro for as long as possible. Though rare, it happens," Tiandra explained.

Riker shook his head. "Guys, that's a reach, don't you think?"

"But your biological mother could've also had other children," Eliana suggested.

"Why are you pushing so hard for a brother?" Riker asked. "We have a witness who says Todd contacted Moneyman the night of the murder. End of story."

"You cannot take Noella's word," Graham said. "She has a lot to lose and who knows if Marvin coerced her."

"As much as I don't want Todd to be innocent, we need the truth, not just pinning whoever is the easiest target," Beckham contended, rejoining the discussion.

"Sorry, Riker, but we agree," Skyler said. "Your biological roots might hold the answer."

"But it doesn't explain why Todd is after me." Riker got to his feet and rubbed the nape of his neck.

"The good news is, Todd's appearance explains why PHACE built the composite." Eliana closed the laptop lid.

"We'll keep digging. Update us when you can," Beckham said, ending the meeting before the group disconnected.

Riker paced around the table. "I should be relieved, but I'm more confused than ever."

"I'm not. We have the who. Todd Billings," Eliana said. "The why is connected to his relation to you." She opened the laptop and her fingers flew across the keys. "Aha!"

"What?"

"Hear me out. I have an idea."

Riker moved behind her, placing one hand on the table. "I'm listening."

"How about a short detour before we head to your parents' home?"

He glanced at the screen, displaying Todd's home address. "No way. Your safety is top priority. I'm not taking you into gang-ridden territory. Who knows what we'll find or what'll find us?" Though Riker couldn't deny his curiosity.

"We should go. Now. What if he's there, clearing out the very evidence needed to exonerate you?"

Riker remained silent, warring within himself.

"Please."

"I'd never forgive myself if something happened to you."

"And I'd never forgive myself if we had this opportunity and didn't take it." She leaned closer, her eyes pleading with him. "I'll do whatever you say. Stay in the car. Sit in a restaurant booth across the street. Even wait at OPD's headquarters. But don't dismiss this."

He groaned. "May I?"

She nodded and he leaned in, studying the screen and mentally mapping the location in his mind. "No. It's too dangerous." He stood and paced a path around the table.

"You said we have to run into the burning building. Offensive."

Pinned by her repetition of his words, he sighed. Was she right?

A cardinal chirped from the tree branch above.

"Fine. But you do as I say. No arguments." He reached for their lunch trash and stuffed it into the bag. "Agreed?"

A slow grin spread over her face. "Yes!" Eliana closed the laptop and gathered her milkshake.

"If the authorities haven't found Todd there, we're wasting our time." Riker's argument sounded weak in his own ears. What was he doing?

"Regardless, we might find clues there," Eliana refuted. "What if he is home?"

"Then we'll detain him until my team arrives to arrest him." Riker stood, second-guessing himself. "I don't know."

"We'll just poke around," Eliana replied, undeterred from her mission. "What's the worst that can happen?"

Riker groaned. "Famous last words."

Once they'd resumed driving, Eliana considered the options. Admittedly, if they found Todd at his house, or discovered any clues that explained his connection to Riker, the visit was worth making. Yet she'd pushed Riker into the idea without notifying his team. Maybe he'd need them as a buffer.

However, Beckham would refuse them permission to make the trip. Better to ask forgiveness.

"Have you considered what seeing Todd face-to-face will do to you?"

Riker flicked a quirked brow in her direction, questioning her comment. "I can handle Todd."

"Emotionally, I mean," she clarified.

A long hesitation said Riker wasn't in agreement. How many times had her motives dictated her actions? How much were they driving her now? Riker had a lot to lose or gain by figuring out Todd's connection to him. And if she was totally honest with herself, she, too, wanted to know.

Never taking his eyes off the road, Riker replied, "Thank you for understanding." He grinned.

She loved his irresistible dimples.

Love? What?

No. Admire. Divert to a different topic. "I have a confession to make. I remembered you'd talked about going into law enforcement in high school, and I kept up with you whenever possible to see if you had."

"You did?"

"Yeah, not in a creepy stalker way," she remarked. "It was neat to see you succeeding at your goals." *And it kept me from telling you the truth about my father.*

"Mom and Dad were proud when I graduated from the academy and joined the state patrol. Later, when I joined the marshals, I think Mom might've hired one of those skywriting planes to announce the news."

"We truly lived in different worlds." *And we still do.* "You must love having a supportive family." Not that she'd experienced that in her life.

"They're the best parents I could ever ask for."

Unable to speak the same about her father, Eliana remained quiet. When Riker offered nothing else, she changed subjects again. "I keep wondering what motivation Todd has to hurt you. If—and I'm not saying he is the one who killed Moneyman—but if it's him, he put a lot of effort into finding the newspaper article, planting evidence, et cetera. Even finding your home residence. That's not a random act of violence."

"Now you're thinking like a cop."

The unexpected compliment melted her, sparking the realization she wanted Riker's approval. When had that happened? "Thank you."

Was it her imagination or had they overcome the dissension that kept them emotionally distant? Though Riker's personal life was being thrust before her, he'd not forbidden her to join him in the journey. That was a huge vulnerability. One she'd still not willingly offered in return to him.

"You went quiet," Riker said, invading her thoughts. "What's on your mind?"

"I appreciate you allowing me to accompany you to your parents' house." She stared out the window. "I mean, you're sort of stuck with me. Even so, it's a big ask to go there, not to mention having a stranger with you for the ride."

"I'm not sure I'd call you a stranger. Though, if you told me more about yourself, that would remedy the issue."

Eliana sighed. Face the inevitable. *Lord, help me word this.* "You asked why I never told you goodbye before we left Lark Point. The truth is, I couldn't. But you should know, I didn't want to go." She watched Riker for a response, but he remained quiet, no doubt waiting for her to continue. She inhaled a fortifying breath. "My father's business forced us to move a lot, so we never stayed in one place very long."

"You were only in Lark Point for that summer," Riker agreed.

"I did get two whole weeks to start school, but yes. Of all

the places we'd lived, Lark Point was my favorite." There were far too many locations Eliana could name that fell in the opposite category.

"Was he in the military or something?"

"I've never told this to anyone." Eliana hung her head, loath to tell him the truth. "No. He, uh, was sort of a salesman."

"And the company he worked for relocated you all often?"

"Not exactly." This was getting more painful by the minute. "My father was a con man."

Riker didn't look at her, but his mouth fell open slightly.

He quickly clamped it shut, and she hurried on before she lost the courage to share the rest. "I didn't realize that until I was much older. He'd come home and demand Hunter and I pack. We never got more than an hour's notice." She picked at her fingernail polish. "I threw a fit the night we moved from Lark Point. That was the only time I'd done that." Eliana didn't add she'd paid greatly for her reaction. "I didn't get to say goodbye to anyone."

Riker reached over, covering her hand, and gently squeezed with reassurance. "Thank you for trusting me with the truth."

His kindness nearly undid her, and the unexpected response surprised her. Relief in releasing the heavy weight she'd carried for so long left her exhausted. "Wish I'd told you sooner."

He gently withdrew and Eliana instantly missed his touch.

"Actually, I'm glad I didn't know." Riker exhaled. "I would've hidden you."

"I might've let you." Except her father had given her the option to stay and never see him or Hunter again. She'd had to go for her brother's sake.

What would it have been like to have someone care for

her? Someone who would be there to hold her while she fell apart? The very idea hurt too much to consider.

"Did your father's nefarious career inspire your development of PHACE?"

She turned away, facing out the passenger's-side window. The reminder acted like a reset button for her mind, propelling Eliana toward the end goal: justice for Hunter.

Eliana crossed her arms over her chest, warding off the vulnerability pressing in on her. She didn't have to tell Riker the details. "When my brother Hunter died, I reprioritized my life. PHACE is the result."

The temporary return to her past reminded Eliana of two things. One, she and Riker lived on parallel planes in very different worlds. She bore the remnants of a criminal father, making her unworthy of a man like Riker. Two, she had to have the task force's endorsement to get Hunter's case reopened. If they convicted Riker of Moneyman's murder, the team would blame her. The media would feast on the story. What was more sensational than a cop gone bad?

Her ultimate goal was to explain the results PHACE provided for Riker. That would help the team take down the actual killer.

"I'm glad you took something bad and turned it for good," Riker said softly.

Eliana studied him, allowing her eyes to travel the contours of his handsome face. She lingered at the structure of his jaw and broad shoulders, then scanned his well-developed biceps, peeking beneath his shirt. Everything about Riker spoke of strength and confidence.

Eliana glanced down at her chipped nail polish. In comparison, she could dress up and disguise her appearance, but the real Eliana Daines was always there, stained and broken beneath the surface. PHACE gave her worth, and that wouldn't happen without the HFTF's endorsement.

Her personal feelings for Riker, whether ancient or new,

were irrelevant and inappropriate. No matter how much time had passed between them, she still felt inadequate around him.

And she still cared for him more than she'd ever confess.

Riker didn't press Eliana for more details about her father, though his cop side wanted to delve into it more. She'd gone strangely quiet, and he felt compelled to break the silence.

"I appreciate you telling me about your dad. My cop radar says there's more that you're not saying. Like why you never contacted me afterward? I would've understood. You were a kid and had to go where your dad took you."

She remained silent. As though that familiar invisible wall had been erected between them again, she'd distanced herself emotionally. Had he said something wrong and offended her?

"How did your brother die?"

Eliana's response said she wasn't going to answer that question. "Both of our careers are on the line with this case."

Riker interpreted this to mean that she wanted him to understand their relationship would remain professional and nothing more. "Agreed. We have a mutual mission to solve Moneyman's murder and get justice. We'll never be safe until we finish this. The sooner we check out Todd's home, the sooner we can get to my parents and put to rest this idea of a twin."

"Or confirm it," she mumbled.

Riker pretended not to hear her. Between worrying about how the visit to his parents would affect them, Todd Billings's involvement and all the questions that brought, and the most recent attacks, Riker's brain was close to short-circuiting.

Eliana was right; he should notify his parents they were coming. He'd never brought a woman home to meet them.

What irony that the first time he did so, she wasn't even his girlfriend. In fact, she might be the catalyst for putting him in prison.

Different worlds. Riker mulled over Eliana's description of their lives. He'd known his own hardships, though admittedly different from hers. She'd had a hard life, and he could only imagine the scars that had left behind. Maybe she saw him as an overbearing cop without a sensitive bone in his body. Or a workaholic. And she'd be correct on both counts. Eliana had already judged him based on the little they knew about one another.

A twinge of conscience pricked at him. Hadn't he done the same? He'd assumed she'd taken off without a backward glance and hadn't cared. He'd nursed a broken and confused heart over his first love, hoping every day for a word from her. Over time, he'd developed his own narrative of the story, assuming she'd found someone better and he'd meant nothing to her. All his presumptions had made sense, considering the other facts he'd added. He'd never once imagined her con artist father had taken her away.

A line had to be drawn in the relationship sand between them. The past put to rest. From here on out, they needed to stick with working the case.

She had established a professional boundary and he'd heed that in total agreement. She'd made it clear she believed in his innocence, yet he longed to pick up where they'd left off. Or start over. Whatever meant Eliana would be in his life. Her return had felt like coming home. How was that possible? Too much time had passed between them, and first love had given way to adult realities.

If they didn't find evidence to exonerate him, he'd face prison for a crime he hadn't committed, while Eliana's business would soar as an acclaimed invention. She'd have immense success while he'd battle for his life every single day in prison.

She remained facing out the window, avoiding him. He had plenty of things to mull over and he needed to do so in the silence of his own mind.

He'd spent the years getting over Eliana, and having the one question he'd hung on to finally answered did absolutely nothing for his heart. She'd kept her distance all these years, then returned for him to help her promote PHACE. But she'd also kept tabs on him. What did that mean? Had grief over the loss of her brother kept her away? If so, why return now? Was he a last resort or just a stepping-stone to where she wanted to go? And why wouldn't she talk about her brother?

They hadn't been together long before she'd left, but the heart didn't require a specified timeline. Riker had fallen hard for Eliana from the first time they'd met. He'd loved no one else because no one else made him feel like Eliana had. No one else compared. For all his training and professional skills, romance was something he'd given up on. Now, he stood falsely accused with everything to lose, all because of a lie that tainted his name with a reputation he hadn't earned.

By the time Riker pulled onto the street where poverty had struck the neighborhood in the harshest ways, he'd exhausted his brain and set his resolve. He had to find Todd Billings and prove he'd set up Riker for Moneyman's murder.

"There's so much sadness here," Eliana said, breaking the silence.

"Yeah. Let's look for a safe place to hide you."

Eliana placed a hand on her forearm. "Please let me go with you."

Why was she so hard to refuse? Though in his care, she'd be safer than left alone to defend herself.

"Fine."

Trash littered the area and homeless people meandered

the street. He scanned the buildings for address numbers until he reached what he assumed was Todd's residence. Riker pulled off to the side, parking near the house but not directly in front of it so as not to draw attention to them. His pickup stuck out like a neon sign in the wounded setting.

"This is it?" Eliana asked.

"I'm surprised the city hasn't condemned this place."

"No kidding."

The run-down clapboard's siding was falling off and a chain-link fence surrounded property where grass had given way to weeds and debris. For a moment, Riker second-guessed his decision, but the demand for the truth and Eliana's persistence overrode his apprehension.

Riker shut off the engine and reached for his gun, tucking it into his waistband. "Stay close to me."

"Believe me, I will."

They exited the vehicle and Riker leashed Ammo before locking the doors. Every instinct blared on high alert as they made their way along the broken sidewalk to the house. He stopped by the black iron mailbox, slanted at an awkward angle, and peered inside. Empty except for several pieces of yellowed junk mail.

"Looks like Todd hasn't been around for a while." Riker held open the gate for Eliana. "Stay behind me."

They stepped through the overgrown weeds to the crooked porch steps where a moth-eaten sofa sat beneath the window.

Ammo whined and Riker wondered if he'd detected explosives. He faced the dog and, offering the hand command, ordered, "Search."

The K-9 sniffed the perimeter, where the windows were barren of screens and several were broken. The house sat between two old brick buildings, crumbling from neglect and long ago abandoned. A stack of junk leaned against the backside of the house and a broken fence revealed the alley. They made their way back to the porch without indication from Ammo.

"Think it's safe?" Eliana asked.

"He hasn't showed any sign otherwise," Riker said as they climbed the porch steps.

The boards beneath them creaked, warning they'd give way under their weight.

Riker kept Ammo close beside him and knocked on the door.

Eliana glanced at him, wariness in her expression. "Um, we're being watched," she whispered.

In Riker's peripheral vision, he spotted a couple of young men walking by, their interest focused on Riker and Eliana. The hairs on his neck prickled. They were sitting ducks exposed on the porch. They needed to get inside. Since it appeared no one had been in the house recently, Riker tested the knob. Unlocked. The door swung open with a screech.

"Act natural, like we belong here."

"Um, isn't this breaking and entering?"

"Probable cause. Ammo was acting strange. Maybe explosives."

"That's a reach."

"Go with it."

They stepped inside, assailed by the stench of trash and urine.

Eliana put a hand over her nose. "Eww."

Stained wood peeked from beneath the ripped shag carpet and an aged sofa with gutted cushions sat against the wall. An old box television set with a hole shot through the middle stood at the opposite side. They crept through the living room to a small kitchen where the refrigerator door hung wide open, permitting a full view of the sparse remains of rotting food. An ancient table leaned heavily on three of its remaining legs.

Ammo sniffed in double-time action. "Poor guy is going

to have olfactory nightmares from this place," Riker said. "Did you know once a dog smells something, the scent is locked in their memory?"

Eliana gasped then coughed and covered her mouth. "Poor Ammo."

Turning the corner, they entered the single bedroom containing an old double bed. A shredded and unkempt quilt partially covered the stained mattress. Opposite the bedroom was a cramped bathroom. The sink and toilet lay on their sides in the filthy tub.

No personal effects were present in the house and anything of worth—had there been any to begin with—were gone.

Ammo moved to the living room window, facing the front yard of the house. His low snarl was unmistakable.

"What's wrong?" Riker inched closer to peer through the window.

Bullets tore through the house in rapid fire from all directions.

Riker tugged Ammo and Eliana to the floor. "Stay down!"

TEN

Mildewy trash odors filled Eliana's senses as she and Riker low-crawled from the room, seeking shelter in the hallway. Gunshots pinged from every side and Riker kept Ammo close as they squatted, arms wrapped over their heads in protection against the raining debris.

"We gotta get out of here!" Riker returned to the low crawl position and Eliana followed suit.

They made their way to the back bedroom, Riker leading. At the window, he rose slowly as bullets continually pelted the front and sides of the house.

"We'll have to climb down that pile of junk."

"Okay." Eliana stood, and Riker helped her through the window. Together, they lowered Ammo outside with Riker exiting last.

Eliana spun, and they sprinted for the six-foot fence barely standing along the back of the yard. They paused beside the open gate.

Riker peered out before waving her through.

Gunfire echoed from the house, propelling her forward.

She followed Riker, ducking and weaving around the dumpsters, old cars and stacks of trash. They stopped at the end of the alley that opened onto a side street.

Pressing against the remnants of a brick building, she asked, "How are we going to get to the truck?"

"Stay here and let me check to see if they're gone."

Eliana listened. The gunfire had ceased.

Riker crept and gestured for her to join him behind a rundown jalopy. They peered over the top as two vehicles screeched away from Todd's house.

Riker and Eliana sprinted toward his truck, which had sustained some cosmetic damage but appeared drivable. They quickly loaded up and Riker shifted in to Drive.

"Ammo, buddy, you just earned yourself a steak dinner for that."

"No kidding." Eliana snapped her seat belt. "Eww, I can't get that smell off me."

"Same here." He rolled down the windows and sped from the neighborhood. Once they were on the highway, he said, "I'd better call it into Walsh."

"Will you tell him where we were before or after telling him the Nites tried to kill us?" she reminded him.

"Ugh. Right."

"Blame it on me. I'm the one who pushed for our visit."

"No. I'll own it. Besides, some good came from the trip. We learned Todd is in trouble with the Nites."

"How do you figure that?" Eliana asked.

"They were watching for Todd to return."

"You ascertained that from our life-threatening visit?"

"The place was deserted, had been picked over, and left uninhabited for an extended period. That tells us Todd's on the run, or he's hiding out," Riker said.

Eliana considered his reasoning, concluding he was right. "Can't argue there. If the Nites believe you killed Moneyman, why would they be after Todd?"

"My first guess is because they think we're the same person," Riker said. "In all seriousness, are you okay?"

"Yeah, I think I'm getting the hang of this running-for-your-life thing," she quipped. "But I respectfully request we drive straight to your parents' house now."

"Most definitely."

Eliana shifted in the seat to get more comfortable. "Todd obviously doesn't have money, so how would he hide?"

"He's a criminal. There's no lack of rocks for him to crawl under."

"Let me play this out." Eliana contemplated her next words. "What if he's on the wrong side of the Nites through no fault of his own?"

Riker snorted. "Are you defending this guy?"

"Not at all. Let's consider all possibilities," Eliana continued, unable to stop herself. "We can't assume he's guilty. Todd could've been an easy target for the Nites."

"And how does that fit into framing me?"

"Hmm. Noella and Marvin exchanged looks. What if he is in on this? Noella could've offered up Todd, and they started a snowball that got out of control."

"Or Todd decided to move himself up the Nites's hierarchy and used me as a stepping-stone," Riker argued.

"If we understood why, that would explain a lot."

They continued debating the possibilities until they reached the South Dakota border.

"Tell me about your folks," Eliana said.

Riker seemed to consider her question. "They're very down to earth."

"And?"

"That's about it."

"Um, I'm assuming you've told them we're co-workers? I'd hate for them to get the wrong impression." Was it her imagination or had a flash of hurt crossed Riker's face?

"I'll make it clear."

"Are you upset with me about something?"

"Not in the least." But his tone and demeanor did not match his words.

By the time they entered Lark Point, the sun hung low in the sky, nestled in the soft glow of pastel oranges, blues and pinks. A series of gorgeous homes lined the Missouri River and Louis and Clark Lake. She'd never been to Riker's home, but Eliana secretly surmised his parents owned the most elaborate one with floor-to-ceiling windows, multiple balconies, a four-car garage and a flowing fountain.

Instead, Riker surprised her by turning in to an older neighborhood with modest homes built in the 1950s or '60s, shifting Eliana's focus.

Riker parked on the narrow driveway of an adorable red-brick bungalow with white trim. Neatly clipped rose-bushes lined the front of the house, and a square concrete patio with three steps led to the door. A yellow glow emitted from inside, visible through lace curtains. Wood flower boxes hung below the windows, housing purple and pink pansies that peeked between creeping Jenny plants that draped to the ground.

Riker turned off the engine.

"Your folks live here?" she asked, amazed.

"Yes. It'll have to do for the night," Riker snapped.

Clearly, she'd offended him. "I didn't mean—"

He exited the truck, ending the conversation, and snagged his duffel bag. Ammo hopped down and Eliana mimicked him, grabbing her laptop suitcase, duffel bag and purse. She stepped away from the truck as a stout, petite woman scurried down the cement porch steps, clinging to the black iron railing. "Riker!"

A man hurried out of the house behind her, wearing an adoring smile.

Riker moved to her side, and released Ammo who barked, tail wagging in recognition.

"Ammo!" The man ruffled the dog's fur. "How's my favorite granddog! I've missed you too."

The woman's face lit with joy as she neared them, and Eliana noticed her stunning silver hair styled in an adorable bob that framed her round face. She pulled Riker into a hug, duffel bag and all. "Am I dreaming? Are you here in person?"

Riker chuckled, his mood opposite from just moments before. "Mom… Mom, let me put my stuff down."

His parents stepped back, smiling, and faced Eliana with curiosity in their expression. Why hadn't she insisted on being dropped off at the nearest hotel? Desperate to become invisible or dissolve into the grass, Eliana clung to her purse.

"This is my work colleague, Eliana Daines. Meet my parents, Lorena and Grady Kastell," Riker said.

Lorena rushed forward, pulling Eliana into a bear hug. "Hello, honey. What a beautiful and unique name. Don't mind us, we're huggers. Come on in!"

Grady gathered her suitcase and duffel. "Let's go inside and you can catch us up."

Eliana trailed behind the group, searching her brain for intelligent icebreakers and feeling self-conscious.

Riker asked, "Is it all right if Eliana takes Isaac's old room?"

"Yes, of course," Lorena gushed. "I'll show you to it."

"Ammo, Poppy has treats for you." His father led the dog into the kitchen.

Eliana awkwardly followed Lorena through the hallway to the first room on the left, where a twin bed positioned against the wall and a small dresser displaying pictures and trophies completed the décor.

"Isaac and Riker were sports fanatics. Don't mind all those."

Eliana placed her bags by the closet, spotting Riker in the doorway.

"Let's get you something to eat." His mother turned and hurried past.

"You could argue, but she'll still make you food." His demeanor had softened.

Had she mistaken his nervousness for standoffishness?

As if understanding her unspoken question, he said, "I'm struggling with this visit."

"I know. Don't worry. I'll smile and nod. Plus, I'm easy to feed," she replied with a grin. "She's too cute."

He nodded.

Grateful he wasn't crabby anymore, she walked with him to the large eat-in kitchen where a table centered the space. Lorena and Grady placed platters of cheese, meat and crackers along with fruit and bread before them. "I'm sorry. I don't have anything fancy on hand," his mother fussily apologized.

"I should've called," Riker said.

Eliana shot him a duh look, to which he mouthed, *I know.*

"This looks delicious. It wasn't fair of us to drop in on you unannounced." Eliana slid into a chair at the furthest end.

Riker sat beside his mother.

"Family doesn't need an appointment," Lorena said. "We're delighted you're here."

His father joined them, passing plates. "We expected you'd show up," Grady said, a serious tone in the softly spoken comment.

Riker's shoulders slumped. "You saw the news?"

"We weren't the first to see the story. Doris called and told us," Lorena said.

Eliana looked at Riker for interpretation.

"She's sort of the town gossip."

"She means well," Lorena replied.

Grady loaded a plate with cheese and fruit, and before the conversation continued, he bowed his head, cueing the rest of them to do the same. He murmured a short grace, to which they all said "Amen."

"This visit has something to do with those false accusations?" Grady then continued.

Eliana blinked. His dad immediately assumed the best

of Riker. What would it be like to have that kind of loving support?

"Yeah. I can't share the details because it's an ongoing investigation." Riker provided a clipped account of the situation, omitting information about the prior death threats and gang attack.

"You're innocent. The truth will come out," his mother assured him.

"Eliana is working toward that goal," Riker said.

With all eyes fixed on her, Eliana gave an abbreviated explanation of PHACE. "I'm wondering if the results are based on a familial connection?"

"Oh, like forensic genealogy?" Grady asked, eyes wide.

Lorena laughed. "He loves crime shows."

"Yes, exactly." Eliana explained her theory of a sibling or lookalike who'd framed Riker for the murder.

"It's no secret we adopted Riker and Isaac. We consider them the most precious gifts God entrusted to us," Lorena said. "But the adoptions were closed, so we have no contact with the birth mother or information on her family."

Eliana's hopes sank, and Riker's countenance must've mirrored her own. Without the familial connection, they had nothing to go off of with Todd Billings. The discussion returned to lighter topics, but Riker wasn't interacting much. Maybe her presence hindered him, especially if there were things about his life he didn't want to share.

"Please excuse me. I'll be right back." Eliana pushed away from the table and walked to the restroom. The rumble of their voices carried to her until she closed the door. Alone, she prayed God would reveal their next steps. And fast.

Riker inhaled, relieved Eliana had gone out of the room. "Truth, son, how're you doing?" His mother pinned him with her tender expression, melting his reserves straight into his boots.

His gaze roved between his parents, but the emotion constricting his throat hindered his response. "I never imagined a false accusation like this would happen to me."

His dad touched his arm. "God will take care of you. He's trustworthy and Jesus knows all about painful false accusations."

Riker bowed his head. "What if I go to prison? How many times have I heard 'I'm innocent' from criminals? I never believed them and all I can think is why would anyone believe me?"

His parents drew closer and prayed aloud over him. The words flowed upon him like warm water and at the collective *Amen*, he absorbed a peace he hadn't felt in a long time. "Thank you," he whispered.

"God is in control, honey. Hold on to that," his mom attested. "On another note, Eliana is beautiful, and she looks so familiar to me."

"She used to live in Lark Point but not for long. Just the summer of our sophomore year and she briefly attended school before she moved," Riker said, trying to ignore the comment. He'd never told his parents about Eliana or the way she'd broken his heart. There didn't appear to be a good reason to share it now, but his father shot him a knowing look.

"Oh, that must be why." His mother nodded. "Is she married?"

"Mom, we're working a case together. That's all." Riker dragged a hand across his chin. "We're not really compatible anyway."

His mom quirked an eyebrow and leaned forward. "If my mom-sense is accurate, you're grouchy and distant, keeping her at arm's length."

Riker gaped. "How do you do that?"

She shrugged. "It's a mother's gift."

"Lorena, leave the boy alone," his father chastised gently. "His vision is fine and I'm sure he's considered the possibilities of a relationship."

"What?" Riker blurted.

Eliana returned. "What did I miss?"

"Nothing." The chime of his cell phone gave him a quick escape. "I need to take this." Ears burning, he moved to the living room and answered. "Hey, boss, what's up?"

"Checking in. Everything all right?" Beckham replied.

"Yes." Riker maintained visual on his parents in case his mother got any more romantic ideas he'd have to run interference on.

"Good. Any leads?"

"Not yet."

"Okay. Don't stay long. You need to get to the cabin."

"Roger that." They disconnected and he returned to his seat at the table.

Eliana and his parents fixed their eyes on him, hope dancing in their expressions. He gently shook his head.

"Eliana, you said you're searching for a familial connection," his dad said.

Riker fidgeted with a cracker on his plate. "I never ask about my adoption. I never cared."

"Wanting the truth isn't something to fear," his dad replied.

"Whoever is framing me looks a lot like me," Riker admitted, unable to shake the disconcerting evidence of Todd's resemblance.

"More than that, PHACE made a DNA connection. Which is why we think he is blood-related," Eliana inserted.

"Understand, we weren't privy to every detail prior to your birth, only that which is applicable to you directly." His mom reached for his father's hand but focused on Riker, kindness crinkling lines around her eyes. "You were a preemie."

"He was?" Eliana asked, her cheeks reddening. "Sorry, didn't mean to just blurt that out."

His father laughed. "It's a valid question. Looking at him now, you'd never believe he started out so tiny."

How had he never known this part of his history?

"You were born with Respiratory Distress Syndrome, admitted to the Neonatal Intensive Care Unit, and kept on oxygen," his mother added.

"Not just a preemie, but a sick one," Riker concluded. "Is that why she gave me away?" The words flew from his mouth before he could stop them. He paused, considering for the first time he'd never allowed himself to think about why he was given up for adoption. Unaware that secret hurt had lain beneath the surface.

"Your birth mother made it clear she surrendered her parental rights due primarily to financial issues," his father interjected. "She simply couldn't afford to care for you and wanted you to have the best."

"Her surrender was an act of love, Riker. And the day they called and said our son was born, a team of football players couldn't have stopped us from rushing to you." His mother's eyes welled with tears and she clamped her hands over his.

"You were the answer to years of prayers," his father said.

"When you love someone, it's hard to let go, even if you know it's better for them," his mother added softly.

"How long was he in the hospital?" Eliana asked.

Her question provided the small reprieve Riker needed to refocus on the investigation.

"Several weeks," his father said. "We stayed by your side every day, singing, talking, playing with you as much as we could through the incubator."

His mother laughed. "At one point, we started including the other babies."

Riker leaned forward, resting his elbows on his knees and intertwining his fingers. "I will have to petition to unseal the adoption records."

"Do you remember anything that might indicate Riker was a twin?" Eliana asked. "Or if he had a sibling, older or younger?"

"No. If his birth mother had surrendered both babies, they'd have notified us." His mother tilted her head, considering the question. "Wouldn't they want to keep them together if possible?"

Riker nodded. The words were confirmation he had no twin. However, it also meant he had no answers to why someone was out to frame him.

"Let me show you pictures." His mother jumped to her feet before anyone responded and hurried from the room.

"Run while you can," Riker teased.

"Nonsense," Eliana said.

"You might regret those words." Riker stood. "We should move to the living room. This could take a while."

His mother was already spreading the albums on the coffee table. "It's been so long since we looked through these." She tugged Eliana beside her on the sofa.

Riker settled next to his father in one of the two recliners. He leaned over and whispered, "How long should I wait before I rescue Eliana from this trip through my childhood?"

Grady chuckled. "You already missed that window, son."

Riker groaned and popped up the footrest. Ammo strolled lazily to his side and lay down, sighing contentedly.

"I love your house," Eliana said, scanning the décor.

"Somehow I figured you would," Riker half joked.

Lorena paused, wide-eyed. "You like the Victorian look too?"

Eliana nodded. "I do."

"Her house looks like yours, Mom," Riker said.

"That proves she's not only brilliant and beautiful, but she has great taste as well," his mom gushed.

Eliana blushed and Riker mouthed, *Sorry*, with a wink, earning him a grin. His mother's observation wasn't wrong.

"Lorena, stop embarrassing the poor woman," his dad interjected.

His mother flipped open a book and pointed to a picture. "Here's Riker on the day we brought him home! Isn't he darling?"

Riker ran a hand over his face and groaned, unable to hide his embarrassment. The women talked easily, as though they'd known one another for years, and Riker couldn't help but notice the tender exchange between them. Eliana fit naturally with his family.

After an hour of his mother's endless cooing about how cute he was, Riker stood. "It's late. We should let you all get some rest."

"Yes, you're right. Eliana, Riker's football trophies are in his old room. They speak for themselves." Lorena sighed and slowly closed the last album. "How long will you be with us?"

"Not sure. I'll call Beckham in the morning. Maybe he's got contacts who'll unseal my adoption records," Riker said. "I'd better take Ammo out once more."

"I wouldn't mind stretching my legs." Eliana got to her feet. "Thank you for a lovely evening."

"Our pleasure," his mom replied.

"Breakfast will be ready when you wake. But enjoy the sleep and don't get up early," his father said.

Riker chuckled. "They're a little bossy," he whispered when they walked out to the backyard. Ammo scurried to do his business then wandered around the lawn. "That was nothing short of awkward. Thank you for being gracious with my mom."

She smiled. "It's clear they adore you."

They moved to the far side of the stone patio, backs

facing the house, and sat on the old wooden bench his dad had refinished.

"Oh, how pretty." Eliana gestured at his mother's pristine garden filled with an abundance of flowering trees in full bloom and perfectly sculpted rosebushes. The soft glow of the porch light illuminated the rows of flowers along the fence.

"My folks love gardening."

"It shows. They're delightful." Eliana scooted back on the bench, bracing her hands on the frame, and swinging her feet lightly. The posture reminded Riker of her younger self.

"They're the best," he agreed. "Honestly, that's why I struggled to come here. I wouldn't hurt them for the world."

"Why would that hurt them?" She turned to face him.

"First, I didn't want to bring danger here. Beckham says we need to get to the cabin ASAP." Riker sighed. "And I didn't want them to think that searching for my birth family meant I'd love them any less."

Kindness shone in her expression. "Your parents don't strike me as easily offended."

"I don't mean it that way." Riker bowed his head, staring at the stone beneath his feet. "It's just they chose me, and I want them to know I choose them too."

"They know." She scooted closer, her leg brushing against him. Her hand covered his, warm and soft.

He looked up, unable to break free from her probing gaze. Their breath mingled with the humid summer air and her nearness overwhelmed him. Riker shifted, facing her. Auburn tendrils framed her face, and he reached to tuck one behind her ear. Eliana tilted her head and glanced down, fluttering her eyelashes. He took in her beautiful features, ignoring his mind's command to stop. The emotions he'd buried for years welled to the surface and Riker allowed himself to feel them.

Eliana raised her eyes, heavy-lidded over the emerald irises that penetrated his heart.

He sucked in a breath and her lips slightly parted.

The back door creaked open and Riker jumped to his feet. His gaze shot from his mother grinning mischievously at him and Eliana studying her fingernails a little too hard.

"Sorry, didn't mean to startle you."

"No problem." Riker rocked on his heels, tucking his hands into his jeans' pockets, aware of the intense burning of his neck and face. Did people spontaneously combust from embarrassment?

"Eliana, towels are in the linen closet inside the bathroom. Help yourself."

"Thank you." Eliana grinned, eyes focused on his mom.

"Good night." She offered a small wave before closing the door.

He moved, leaning over the back of the bench, his cheek close to Eliana's. "Don't turn around, but she's watching through the window."

Eliana snickered. "You're certain?"

"I wish I wasn't." He grumbled playfully. "Thank you for coming with me and enduring the mountains of pictures." Riker returned to sitting beside her.

"I loved it." She lifted a leg and tucked her foot under her thigh.

"I should visit more." Riker brushed the grass with his boot. "When I have time off work, I like to go to the cabin my brother and I share."

Eliana frowned slightly. "Wow, I really judged you all wrong. I assumed you were rich."

He chuckled. "Apparently, you haven't seen the pay scale for the US Marshals."

She blinked. "Now that you mention it, no."

"The Dundee house belonged to my grandfather and, after his death, the place sat empty until the city condemned the property. As soon as I could afford it, I bought the house to keep it in the family. I've spent years in renovations and, truthfully, it's my love-hate project. I'm nowhere close to finished, but at least it's inhabitable."

"The house is incredible. You did all the renovations?" Eliana's eyes widened.

"Yes. It's a hobby slash time killer slash stress reliever. My paternal grandfather gave my brother, Isaac, and me the Valentine hunting cabin. We worked on restoring that together."

"I can't wait to see it." Eliana yawned. "Sorry."

"No, it's late and we didn't get much rest last night. Let's head inside."

Ammo sauntered up to them, satisfied with his inspection of the yard.

"See, he's tired too," Riker quipped, leading them into the house.

"Good night." Eliana walked past him and headed into the hallway.

Riker moved to his old bedroom, where time had stood still. All the trophies and books remained in the same place. He lifted a picture of his high school youth group. He and Eliana sat side-by-side on the church stoop, both grinning wide. The happiest day of his young life. Should he tell her the truth about his feelings?

What difference would it make now? They were getting along and, after the investigation, they'd return to being co-workers and nothing more. He set the frame on his nightstand and turned off the light.

Some secrets should remain secrets.

ELEVEN

A soft brush against her forehead and a man's voice invaded Eliana's dreams.

"Eliana, wake up."

She groaned, unwilling to awaken until a hand touched her arm, giving it a gentle shake. Eliana forced open her eyes, adjusting to the dim light, then started awake at the form standing over her. She scrambled back against the headboard, tugging the blankets higher.

"Don't scream. It's just me. Riker." Raised hands combined with the familiar voice calmed Eliana and she blinked to clear her vision.

Riker stepped to the side and warned, "I'm going to turn on the light."

"Okay," she croaked, squinting against the baseball lamp's sudden illumination.

"I was trying not to scare you."

"You did a lousy job," she mumbled. "What time is it?" She reached for her cell phone on the nightstand, remembering too late she'd tossed the device in exchange for the cheap burner phone.

"Two twenty a.m., we have to leave ASAP."

"Why?" Eliana sat up, rubbing the sleep from her eyes. "What's wrong?"

"Beckham called and said intel shows the Nites are

headed this way. My parents are in danger, so he's relocating them. You and I must go too."

Riker's words fluttered around her brain, searching for a place to land as she struggled to comprehend what he'd just said. She started to push off the sheets, then thought better of it since she was only wearing her nightshirt.

"I'll meet you in the living room. Wheels up in ten." He exited the room, closing the door softly behind him.

Thrusting her foot out, she slid from the bed, already missing the warmth and the refreshing sleep. When was the last time she'd gotten a full eight hours of rest? She reached for her bag and dragged out fresh clothes, including a pair of jeans and her favorite T-shirt, then slipped into socks and running shoes. Though she tried to move stealthily and not make a ton of noise, her exhausted state left her unstable, and she teetered into the dresser.

"Ouch," she whisper hissed, rubbing the sting from her shoulder. Stuffing her belongings into her bag, she double-checked the room to ensure she hadn't forgotten anything, then toted her bags into the living room.

Riker and his parents spoke quietly and glanced up at her approach. Lorena and Grady were also dressed, and their suitcases sat near the door.

"Beckham's ETA is five minutes," Riker reported.

"I'm sorry we have to leave like this," Eliana said.

"It might have to get worse before it gets better," Lorena replied.

Eliana crossed the room and placed her bags beside the front door. She dropped into the recliner nearest Riker.

"We understand the demands of Riker's job," Grady explained. "Commander Walsh has always been trustworthy, so if he says it's time to go, we won't argue. Besides, this might be a new adventure for us." He pulled Lorena close in a sideways hug.

"Promise when this is over, you'll both come back again?"

Eliana spotted the slight quiver in Lorena's brave smile. As much as she wanted to agree, how could she? She had no privilege or right to return to their home once the case was resolved. And if the end results didn't favor Riker, the Kastells wouldn't want her there.

"Please?" Lorena pressed.

"I'd love to." No lie there.

"Good." Satisfied, she withdrew from her husband's embrace. "Oh, let me pack something for you to eat on the road." She scurried into the kitchen before anyone had a chance to protest.

"In that case—" Eliana stood "—I'd like to use the restroom before we go."

"You've got a few minutes," Riker replied.

Grady chuckled. "You're not leaving until your mother has given you enough food to feed a small army."

"I heard that," Lorena called.

The light banter endeared the Kastells even more to Eliana and she hurried to the bathroom, struggling to catch a calming breath. The few seconds to clean up and splash water on her face helped her to fully awaken, but her reflection in the mirror testified to hours of missed sleep. There wasn't time to remove the exhausted evidence from her face and she returned to the living room.

Riker peered out the side of the curtains as Lorena emerged from the kitchen. She crossed the room and handed Riker a large, insulated bag. "It's not much, but it'll keep you from going hungry on the way."

"Thanks, Mom." He kissed her cheek.

Ammo sidled up beside them, tail wagging.

"Don't worry, I'd never forget to include treats for my favorite granddog," Lorena said. "There's something in there for him too."

Ammo gave a soft woof of appreciation, eliciting a chuckle from the group.

"I guess his hearing isn't as bad as the vet said." Grady winked.

Riker petted the dog. "I think he has more selective hearing these days."

"I'll carry the food," Eliana offered, taking the bag from him.

Lights beamed from outside.

"Beckham is here." Riker opened the front door, hoisting the duffel on to his shoulder and taking Eliana's bag. "I'll make another trip to get the rest."

Grady walked to the kitchen and returned carrying two travel mugs, one printed with Best Mom, the other with Greatest Dad. "You'll need the caffeine."

Stunned by the thoughtfulness the Kastells offered, Eliana reached to take the mugs, but Grady shook his head. "I'll carry them out for you."

"Thank you." She collected her laptop bag and trailed behind Ammo and the men.

Lorena gently touched Eliana's arm, stopping her. "Forgive me for overstepping, but I need to say this."

Eliana nodded, dreading the next words. Would Lorena berate her for Eliana's unprofessionalism after catching them last night on the back patio? Maybe Lorena assumed they'd kissed? Truthfully, Eliana wished they had, but that would only complicate matters, and their lives were a tangled web of complex issues already.

"Riker can be difficult and crabby," she said. "But there's so much more under the grumpy exterior. He's a good man and he loves the Lord. I suppose every mother says that about her child."

"I understand," Eliana said even though she didn't.

Lorena pulled her into a hug. "God's got this."

Touched by the kindness, Eliana searched her brain for

the right words to speak. Instead, she relaxed in the unfamiliar motherly embrace. Being held made her want to reveal her own wounds, needing that maternal comfort. Something Eliana had never known after her mother passed away and she'd longed for every single day since. Lorena didn't release her hold for several seconds, as though she understood the unspoken need.

The front door opened, and Riker entered, a look of curiosity in his furrowed brow.

Lorena stepped back, wiping the moisture from her cheeks. "I warned you, we're huggers."

"It's nice." Eliana forced a smile, absorbing the acceptance. These people had welcomed her into their home without judgment or question. Had Riker told them they'd dated briefly in high school? What would they think of her if they discovered the truth about her upbringing and life? She blinked back tears. "Thank you for the kind hospitality. I truly enjoyed the visit."

Lorena smiled. "Anytime. We loved meeting you and look forward to seeing you again."

If PHACE became the catalyst for Riker's prison sentence, they'd rescind their offer. Once more Eliana prayed for the truth to come out, exonerating Riker from charges. "I'd like that."

"Ready?" Riker lifted the last of the bags and Lorena rushed to shut off the lights.

"Yes." Eliana followed him outside and down the steps.

Lorena locked the front door and then hurried to join Grady, standing beside the SUV with Beckham, their voices low and serious. Riker's pickup engine rumbled and Ammo hung his head out the back window, tongue lolling. Beckham took the Kastells' bags from Riker. "I was just telling your father how sorry I am to do this to them."

"No, we understand," Grady replied.

Lorena touched Riker's cheek. "We'll see you soon."

"I'll be the one to bring you home when this mess is over," he promised.

"We love you beyond words." His mom and dad embraced Riker and prayed over him.

Not a single recollection surfaced for Eliana of her father treating Hunter or her that way. Had her mother lived, she probably would've. The bitterness that accompanied so many of Eliana's painful memories lingered.

"I love you both." The pain in Riker's voice tore at Eliana's heart.

He trailed his parents to Beckham's SUV and helped them inside. Eliana took the opportunity to load herself into the pickup, stroking Ammo's head before settling into her seat.

As though the world had shifted dramatically, Eliana resolved to do whatever it took to help Riker. She'd lay down her own dreams. She refused to be the reason he went to prison. How could she possibly live with herself if that happened? He had a family; wonderful parents who loved him. Unlike Eliana. She had no one. Even solving Hunter's case would do nothing to bring back her brother. And though she longed to ensure his killer was held accountable, Riker needed her. And the truth was, she needed him too.

Beckham was already driving away by the time Riker slid behind the wheel.

"Will you be told where they are?" Eliana asked.

Riker worked his jaw and shifted into Drive. "No. It's safer if I'm not aware of their location." After several beats, he admitted, "I hate this."

"I know." She lifted a hand to offer a supportive touch, but his off-putting glance had her withdrawing.

The pain that flickered in his blue irises nearly undid her but something else lingered there. Did he blame her for this most recent development? Eliana averted her eyes, shifting her hands into her lap. And why shouldn't he? Wasn't she the one who'd pushed him to come here? Wasn't she responsible for endangering his parents?

"Riker, I'm sorry." When he didn't immediately respond, she bit her lip and prepared for a lashing. "I don't blame you for being mad at me."

"It crossed my mind, but the truth is none of this is your fault," Riker said. "The Nites are merciless. The killer placed the news article picture in Moneyman's jacket to remind me that my parents were a target too."

"A veiled threat we didn't pick up initially?" Eliana asked.

"I considered the possibility but hoped otherwise." Riker sighed, working his hands over the steering wheel. "That was idiotic on my part."

"It's been a long time since I had anyone else to think about, but I do remember what it's like to want to protect the ones you love." She considered the numerous times Riker had risked his life for her. "You deserve the truth." Picking at her nail polish, she worked up the courage to speak. "I told you my brother died."

"I'm sorry for your loss." Riker's tone held compassion in the familiar condolence she'd heard over the years.

"I didn't tell you how. He was shot and killed. At the time, technology was insufficient for finding his killer. His case remains unsolved."

"That's terrible."

Eliana stared at the yellow lines on the highway. "Losing Hunter made me reprioritize my life. I had to find a way to honor him. The good part that came from it all was developing PHACE."

"What happened to your father?"

Eliana sighed, not wanting to share the bitter details, but she'd come this far and there was no turning back. "He took off. Never said goodbye or anything. One day I got home after work and all his things were gone. I learned of his death a year later."

This time, Riker reached out, placing a hand over hers. The powerful moment grounded her, providing stability for her emotions that threatened to go haywire. "You've been on your own ever since?"

Unable to speak, she nodded.

"Eliana, I had no idea."

She forced away the tears welling in her eyes before responding. "My past is humiliating."

"Why? None of that was your fault."

"Because right, wrong or indifferent, everyone judges to some degree."

Riker withdrew his hand, gripping the wheel again. "I'm guilty of that. After years of law enforcement, I've seen too much of humanity's ugliness. But now, I find myself reconsidering how judgmental I was toward criminals. I never granted anyone else the benefit of the doubt, or mercy in my thoughts. And here I am hoping the authorities will somehow see me differently."

"We're both getting a lesson in judgment."

"Definitely."

Reminded of her goals, Eliana made her final plea and admission. "If I do nothing else with my life, I want to help solve Hunter's murder."

Riker flicked a glance her way. "How?"

"I'd like to run the evidence through PHACE. Except I need your team's endorsement to prove to Denver PD that the system is legitimate." She held her breath. Would he explode at the request? Assume she'd used him?

"I think that's a noble goal."

She blinked several times, uncertain she'd heard him correctly. "There's more."

"Okay."

"I'm committed to helping you. As much as I want Hunter's case solved, you must be exonerated."

His forced laugh spoke volumes about his mindset. "I haven't been charged. Yet."

"We'll solve your case before they get a chance to do that." Eliana twisted in her seat and blurted the rest. "Whatever it takes, I will help you find the truth." And whatever that truth revealed, she'd find a way to keep him from going to jail. "Even if it costs me everything."

"No." Riker stared into the windshield, debating if he'd misunderstood Eliana. Was she saying she'd sacrifice her career, her life, for him?

"No what?"

"I won't contribute to you losing one more thing. I understand your desire to solve Hunter's case. If you'll let me, I'd like to help."

"After we finish yours," she stated.

"Or before," Riker contended. "I mean it. I'm in."

She shifted, blinking fast, as if she was overcome, then said, "Okay. You have no idea how much I appreciate this, Riker."

He glanced into the rearview. Ammo had curled up in his favorite place on the seat next to the door. "He's out for the count."

"I'm ready to join him."

He'd find a way to handle all of it and get his parents home safely. The need to be honest with Eliana wore on his defenses. She'd revealed her heart, and his mom's voice poked at his conscience. "I have a confession of my own."

That got her attention. "You do?"

Contemplating how much he wanted to share, he concluded it was only fair to tell her the truth, as she'd been with him. "I haven't treated you fairly."

"I wouldn't say that. Exactly." Her lips curved upward mischievously.

"When you contacted me out of the blue, I wasn't happy."

"I gathered that."

"I figured my team would refuse to beta test PHACE."

"Ah." She pressed a finger against her temple. "So that's why you had me contact Beckham directly."

He winced. "Yeah."

"Because you were angry that we moved without me telling you goodbye or getting in touch afterward?"

Riker groaned. "Since you've shared the background, I feel really dumb admitting that."

"No. I get it." Eliana shrugged. "I wish I'd handled things differently too."

"There's more." Riker sucked in a breath. "I was hurt when you left, but we were just kids in high school and, looking back, I admit it was a summer romance. When you called me about PHACE, I was annoyed because you hadn't bothered to contact me any time before then. I felt used." Eliana started to speak and he said, "Wait. Let me finish, please."

She nodded.

"I understand why you did what you did. And I'm grateful you thought of me, especially with all you have riding on it. But your return triggered emotions I didn't expect."

"Now I'm intrigued."

"I've never had a serious relationship. I dated some, but nothing long term." *Because no one compared to you.* Riker inhaled, averting his eyes, afraid he'd spill his feelings if he saw any hope in her eyes. *Keep to safer topics.* "Instead, I focused on football. You noticed I didn't want to talk about my athletic achievements when my mom brought them up?"

"Yeah, but I figured you were humble or tired." She snickered.

"Both," he chuckled. "If it were up to me, those would've been packed away a long time ago," Riker said. "I had big dreams of going pro, but that didn't happen."

"I'm listening."

"I ate, drank and breathed football all through high school, and it got me scholarships into college. I wasn't into partying or chasing girls. I had to maintain my grades, and between classes and practice, I had little time to do much of anything else." Riker hesitated to remember the incident that tore down his dreams. "The big game where several football talent scouts attended, I broke my leg in three places and got a serious concussion. The injury took me out for the rest of the season and the doctor warned I could permanently damage my brain if I kept playing."

"Did your parents make you quit?"

"No. They're not like that." He sighed. "They talked with me extensively about the pros and cons, and ultimately agreed it was my life and I had to make up my own mind."

"They stood beside you and I'm guessing they would have regardless," Eliana said.

"Probably. My dreams were crushed, and I didn't know what to do. I'd toyed with going into law enforcement but hadn't really committed to it. I felt like everything I had worked for was stolen from me."

"That's awful." Eliana tucked her foot under her thigh. "You turned a disappointment into a wonderful career, though."

"Yeah, and now I might have those dreams destroyed again. I'm tired of having the rug ripped out from under me after I've worked hard to achieve something." The confession released some of the tension in his shoulders.

"It's hard not to put our worth into our careers." Eliana glanced down.

Like a two-by-four upside his head, Riker realized he'd done the same thing. *Lord, forgive me.* "If my mom was here, she'd say our worth comes from God alone." He gave Eliana a sideways grin.

"Ouch. She's right. I guess I put too much of my value into what happened with PHACE." She paused. "I've al-

ways believed that getting closure for Hunter would bring
me peace. But what if it doesn't?"

"Ah, now here, my mom would add 'peace comes from
trusting God regardless of circumstances,'" Riker replied
softly.

"She's wise."

His heart warmed at Eliana's words. "Funny how those
little phrases come back to my memory so fast." Changing
topics, he said, "PHACE is revolutionary and could be a
huge help to our team and other law enforcement agencies.
I'll talk with Beckham about the endorsement."

"Thank you, Riker." She gently touched his forearm.

Combined with the way Eliana spoke his name and her
gentle touch, Riker's mouth went desert dry.

"We've got no lack of things to work on. First, I want
to figure out the coding that's causing the false results in
your case."

"Right," he finally croaked. "Unless Todd Billings is
my twin brother, and he really is determined to kill me or
have me killed."

"Well, that is a huge factor," she admitted, tongue in
cheek.

He might run out of time to help Eliana if Todd got his
way. "Could you dial Beckham's number for me and put
it on speaker?"

"Sure." She straightened in her seat, then reached for
his phone and made the call.

"Riker, is everything okay?" Beckham asked after the
first ring.

"Yes. So far, it's quiet. You're on speakerphone since
we're driving," Riker said.

"Good. Just secured your parents too." Beckham sighed.
"I'm truly sorry it's come to this."

"We'll win this, boss." Riker stared at the dividing highway lines, then said, "I have a couple of big asks."

"Go ahead."

"Would you contact Denver PD on Hunter Daines's homicide cold case?" Riker asked. "We're hoping they'll provide a DNA sample from the evidence so Eliana can run it in PHACE."

Eliana jerked to look at him, her mouth set in an *O*.

"Daines. Related to you, Eliana?" Beckham inquired.

"Yes," she squeaked, then explained, "Hunter is my brother. He was shot and killed ten years ago."

"Absolutely. I'll make some calls."

"Thanks." Riker exhaled and said, "Also, do you have any contacts in the judicial system who might unseal my adoption records? The normal process takes too long. We need to know if Todd Billings is my twin."

"Your folks weren't able to provide any information?"

"Nothing that would explain the twin situation."

"I'll get on it," Beckham replied, enthusiasm in his tone. "Skyler and Tiandra will meet you at the cabin by noon."

"Roger that." Riker disconnected.

"Thank you seems sadly deficient in expressing my appreciation," Eliana said, a quiver in her voice.

"Not sure what we'll get, but it won't be for lack of trying."

She nodded. "Feels like we've been driving for hours."

"Close." Riker shifted topics with her.

"Where are we?"

"Somewhere between no-man's-land and in-the-middle-of-nowhere," he teased.

She chuckled. "Right." She leaned back and closed her eyes. "Mind if I doze for a bit?"

"Not at all."

Riker crested a hill an hour later and the low fuel light warning chimed on the dashboard. He spotted a sign for the next off-ramp and merged off the highway. But when no gas station appeared, he debated whether he'd exited

too soon. Finally, a mile further down the road, he saw a
mom-and-pop station on the right side, hidden beneath an
overgrowth of trees and tall grass.

Referring to the decrepit building as a gas station might
be a stretch. Its best days had long since passed, and though
a light glowed from inside, no other vehicles testified to the
presence of humans. Riker glanced down at the gas gauge
hovering in the vicinity of fumes, and prayed the pump had
a credit card payment option.

Cloudy skies hindered the morning sunrise, and the
heavy tree cover shadowed the wooden structure. Riker
pulled up to the aged single pump and searched for pay-at-
the-pump signs. Locating none, he sighed and glanced over.
Eliana breathed softly, confirming she was still asleep. Neither of them had gotten much rest in the past couple days.
He determined to fuel up and then take Ammo for a short
walk without waking her.

Ammo poked his head between the front seats.

Riker stroked his velvety ears. "Stay and guard," he
whispered, reiterating the command with accompanying
hand gestures. Tail thumps confirmed his K-9 understood.
He slid from the vehicle, depressing the locks before gently
shutting the door.

He studied the pump once more and, validating there
was no credit card option, turned and strode to the building. His gaze roved the area for any trouble. Birds trilled
above and two squirrels chased each other from tree to tree.

A foot from the door, he caught sight of the handwritten
sign taped to the dingy glass. *Back at 8:15 a.m.* He glanced
at his watch. Not for another couple of hours. Riker reached
for the handle, finding it unlocked. Unsurprising as rural
businesses still held to the trust policy, especially considering the location of this place. They probably didn't get
many visitors or customers. He entered and spotted several
rows of shelves proudly displaying candy and gum along

with other munchie foods. How long had some of it been there? He didn't want to know.

"Hello?" He made his way through the strange rectangular space before returning to the front. Satisfied no one was working, Riker placed cash on the yellowed counter then returned to the truck.

Ammo watched from the passenger window.

Riker began fueling the vehicle, listening to the slow rhythmic glugs. He moved around the backside of the pickup, surveying the area. A click sounded, confirming the tank was full. He replaced the nozzle, unlocked the doors with his key fob and released Ammo.

The K-9 jumped down and gave a thorough shake.

Eliana glanced his direction, bleary-eyed. "Hey," she rasped.

"I was going to let you rest."

"Hmm…'kay," she mumbled, closing her eyes and leaning her head against the seat.

"I'll walk Ammo quickly. Be right back." He watched her and she gave an almost imperceptible nod. "I'll walk you to the gas station, if you need a break. There's no one working, but the door is open, so we can use the restroom."

Eyes still closed, her breathing returned to the soft rhythmic sounds of sleep.

"Keep the doors locked." Riker repeated, "I'll be right back."

She didn't respond.

Riker closed and locked the door, then snapped on Ammo's leash. Eliana had slid down in the seat, laying her head on the console. In her position, she was hidden from anyone driving on the road.

Ammo tugged on his leash, eager to move. Riker headed away from the truck into the tree line, allowing him to wander into the wooded area. He relished the walk and fresh air. They both needed the break.

Riker stretched the ache in his back but couldn't shake off the unease that clung to him. He'd grown used to life-threatening events on a regular basis and the quiet was almost more unnerving.

Ammo sniffed around an old maple tree, taking his time.

Lack of sleep had worn down Riker's defenses, and his emotions rode on the edge. They'd taken an alternative path, using county roads and little traveled highways to make their way from his parents' house just north of the Nebraska/South Dakota border. Was that enough to shake the killer?

Ammo strained on his leash, wanting to explore further into the tree line. With one last glance at the pickup, Riker rounded the building, reassuring himself no one was around. Besides, even if a car approached, he'd hear and quickly return to Eliana.

They needed to get to the cabin. He'd rest up then be at the top of his game. Once there, he could relax.

They were almost in the clear.

TWELVE

Eliana shifted and groaned, easing herself upright in the seat. She cringed at the pins-and-needles sensation of her left arm, numb from the way she'd slept on the console. With her right hand, she massaged the unbearable ache in her neck while acclimating herself. Morning sunlight peeked through the heavy cloud cover above and the overcast sky dimmed the surrounding scenery. Where were Riker and Ammo? A vague recollection of talking to Riker bounced to the forefront of her mind but revealed nothing pertinent to the moment.

Or had she dreamed the whole thing?

Soft light glowed from the dilapidated building across from her. Perhaps he'd gone inside with Ammo? She released her seat belt, then unlocked and pushed open the door to gain a better view of her surroundings. The thick wooded area provided ample exploration opportunities, and she silently reassured herself that Riker had taken Ammo for a short walk.

Eliana stepped out of the truck and stretched her arms before rolling her neck to work out the kinks. She considered calling out for him, but there wasn't another vehicle or human in sight. Besides, they'd driven for hours, and she needed to use the restroom. One more visual assessment determined no potential dangers, so she headed for the building.

The scent of impending rain hung in the air, and songbirds chirped cheerfully from the trees. Before she reached the front door, a note taped to the glass caught her eye. *Back at 8:15 a.m.* Eliana never wore a watch, so she had no clue what time it was, but surely, they'd allow her to use the restroom. Besides, there was no one to ask permission.

She stepped inside. "Riker?"

No response.

She crossed the room, spotting money on the counter, evidence Riker had been there. She walked to the far side and pushed open the door marked Restroom. Double stalls and a small pedestal sink comprised the clean albeit dated space. The door slammed behind her with a thud, startling her.

Eliana entered the first stall and slid the dingy green metal lock in place.

A click and the lights went out, thrusting her into darkness. Eliana's hands moved across the cold metal in search of the lock. At last, finding it, she jerked open the door and stepped out. Arms outstretched, she felt her way forward. Her fingertips grazed fabric.

"Peekaboo." The man's low voice turned Eliana's blood to ice.

A small exit sign glowed green, but the black balaclava disguised the assailant's face.

Before Eliana's scream erupted, he grabbed her hair and slammed her against the wall. The force sent tiny flickers of light dancing in front of her eyes, disorienting her.

He shoved her, and she stumbled backward.

"Help!"

The man swept her feet out from beneath her. Eliana smacked her head against the sink before landing hard on her left side. She gasped, fingers clawing at the cold linoleum tile. A kick to her chest flattened Eliana on her back.

The world spun and she struggled to regain her breath.

In a flash, he pressed his full weight down on her torso, hindering her breathing. Beefy hands encircled her throat as he squeezed the air from her lungs, threatening to crush her windpipe.

Eliana fought, twisting and kicking, but he was much larger, and she struggled under his bulk. The desperation to breathe overruled everything else. Her vision adjusted to the darkness and her eyes frantically surveyed the space, searching for the exit.

His grip tightened. If she didn't fight, he'd kill her.

God, give me strength. Eliana thrust her hips upward, throwing the man off balance. He teetered to the right, and she rolled from under him. He lunged again, but Eliana jumped out of his reach. She kicked, landing a foot to his face.

He yowled and fell onto his behind. Eliana bolted from the restroom. She opened her mouth to scream, but her throat failed to comply. She flung open the door and sprinted outside.

She tried to cry out again, succeeding. "Riker! Ammo!"

A barked response sent her scurrying around the backside of the building.

"Eliana!"

Dog and man emerged from the tree line. Ammo growled, straining against his leash toward the building.

"A man attacked me!" Eliana heaved, hand clutching her sore throat.

Riker jerked to look past her. "In the truck?"

"No, inside the gas station."

Without a word, Riker and Ammo hurried inside, Eliana trailing.

"He's gone," Riker said. "Are you okay?" His face had reddened and his blue eyes darkened.

"Yeah." Eliana surveyed the interior. "Do you think they have cameras?"

Riker quirked an eyebrow and gestured toward the run-down building. "I'm guessing no, but we'll contact them just in case."

"I'm pretty sure it was the same guy who broke into my house."

Riker's pinched lips conveyed his understanding. Nelson's shooter. He glanced down at Ammo, gave the hand command, and ordered, "Hunt."

Eliana stayed close to the team as they exited the gas station and moved around the other side of the building into the trees, opposite to where Riker and Ammo had been.

At the far end of the property, two immense round hay bales concealed a compact toolshed. Ammo paused beside it, and Eliana spotted tire tracks in the dirt. "Why wouldn't we have heard an engine?"

Riker knelt to inspect the ground. "These tires are small, but a car, not a motorcycle or UTV. Maybe one of those hybrid type of vehicles."

"Like an electric car?"

"Exactly. They're silent for the most part, so who knows how long the culprit had been here." He glanced at Ammo. "Which explains why he wouldn't have heard it." His tone was apologetic.

"None of us did." Eliana knelt and petted the sweet dog. "However, he barked when I screamed."

"That's right," Riker said as though relieved. "He was sniffing to his heart's content, then suddenly spun around and bolted toward the gas station." Stroking the dog, Riker praised him. "You did good, buddy."

Eliana got to her feet. "Let's get out of here. Except, would you mind guarding the bathroom for a minute?"

Riker chuckled. "Absolutely."

When Eliana emerged from the restroom, Riker and Ammo stood at the storefront. "I updated Beckham. He'll contact the owners of the store and see about cameras and notify them of the events. He agrees we need to get some place safe."

"Sounds good to me." They exited the building. "How do we know he's not following us again?"

"I watched for vehicles on the way here. There wasn't a soul for miles." Rider passed her Ammo's leash. "Before you get in the truck, let me inspect for a GPS tracker or incendiary device."

Eliana nodded and kept a distance while Riker circled the vehicle, searching the tires and body, even under the hood.

"I'm not finding anything." Riker opened both passenger doors, and she climbed inside while he loaded Ammo.

Within minutes, they were on the road again. "Riker, was the threat against your parents a ruse to divert our attention?"

"You reason like a cop," he said. "And yes, I considered that, too. Although he couldn't have known where I'd pull over for gas. He's gutsy and not afraid to attack, but is it my imagination, or does it seem like he's afraid of Ammo?"

"Now that you mention it, he disappeared when Ammo barked in reply to my cries."

"He could shoot my dog, but he doesn't. At my house, when he attacked me, he left Ammo locked inside my vehicle. And whenever Ammo's present, like at your house and again in the restroom, he flees." Riker's mind swirled with contrasting thoughts. "Or maybe he's a wimp and can't tackle us both, so he takes one swing at a time."

"None of this makes any sense to me," Eliana said. "But it's getting old." She rubbed the place where a throbbing headache intensified by the minute.

"On second thought," Riker said, glancing over, "you need to be examined by a doctor. You could have a concussion."

"No way. I'm fine." Eliana put her hands in her lap, emphasizing her words. "Let's just get to the cabin."

"I don't know..."

"Really. I promise, if I have any weird symptoms, I'll tell you." Eliana reached for the travel mug and sipped the tepid coffee. "What if he tracks us there too?"

"We're taking an alternative route and I'll change vehicles with Tiandra," Riker said, reaching for his phone. "I don't think he can trace the cabin to me since the property is under my brother's name, although this guy has proved he's savvy." Riker's cell phone rang. "Please answer it on speakerphone."

"Sure." Eliana grabbed the device and hit the button.

"Hey, boss, I really miss my old phone."

"We'll get new ones reissued soon," Beckham said. "Where are you?"

"Just outside Valentine. I need to trade vehicles before we head to the cabin."

"Graham will swap SUVs with you in O'Neill. Then meet with Skyler and Tiandra at Smith Falls," Beckham advised. "I'll have backup at the cabin and will order them to patrol the area."

"Roger that."

A click confirmed Beckham had disconnected. She'd never get used to the abbreviated way they communicated.

Riker faced her. "Guess we're taking a minor detour."

"Is that normal?"

"Nothing about this case has fallen in that category," he said, turning around.

Unease hung between them as both watched for tails. But the rural roads were lightly traveled and mostly by semitrucks.

When Riker pulled into the town of O'Neill, he headed for a beautiful old church. He pulled around to the back, where Graham sat waiting in a tan SUV.

The interaction was short as they transferred vehicles.

"I'll follow you at a distance and flash my headlights if

I see anything," Graham said. "If that happens, take a detour and we'll meet up again at Smith Falls."

Within minutes, they were en route again. Riker made several turns, and they traveled a country road that transitioned between gravel and pavement.

Eliana sighed, fixating on the incredible scenery around her. Lush, green growth bordered both sides of the two-lane paved road. Overhead, cerulean sky peeked through the white fluffy clouds that had replaced the darkening atmosphere.

They parked at a welcoming center building beside a pickup Eliana recognized as belonging to Tiandra.

Graham pulled in behind them and rolled down the driver's window. "I'll watch here until you're done. Beckham's already checking out the cabin."

"Thanks." Riker leashed Ammo, and they proceeded through the visitor area to a staircase that led down a rocky path.

"This is so pretty," Eliana said, scanning the picturesque scenery where the grass stretched wide to the flowing river. Rich foliage and sparse wildflowers covered the rolling hills on either side of them.

"It's a hidden beauty," Riker agreed.

The red-rock path led to a bridge made of wood and iron that reached across the rushing water. Intrigued, she spotted a small sign that read Verdigre Bridge, captioning the history of the structure. They crossed the bridge and Eliana paused to peer down into the murky depths. The scenery infused her with peace, and she felt her body relax in the soothing atmosphere. "I could stay here forever."

"Wait until you see the falls."

Along the walking path, she spotted an oversized blue frame with the words "Smith Falls State Park," which offered the opportunity to capture their visit with a photo memory.

Eliana's joy faltered and she hesitated, staring at the image. How long would they be on the run? Would she ever know a carefree life again?

She glanced up and noticed Riker watching her. His forehead creased with concern. She quickly plastered a smile on her face and joined him alongside a second wooden walkway with railings. Trees and bushes heavy with leaves in varying shades of green bordered both sides. The sound of running water grew louder as they walked deeper between the towering earthen walls.

Eliana gasped as they rounded the corner. Ahead, an enormous waterfall gushed from over sixty feet above to the small rocky pool beneath.

Skyler and Tiandra stood at the edge of the walkway, while Bosco wandered around the water below.

"We knew you'd lose reception once you reached the cabin, so we opted to meet here beforehand," Skyler explained.

Tiandra added, "We already checked the cabin for you, and Beckham's there, so you're good to go."

"Good thinking." Riker released Ammo, and he hurried to join his canine companion.

"We also brought you new cell phones to replace those burner ones," Skyler said, handing Eliana and Riker the devices. "Although I'm not sure how much good they'll do you."

"It's like having an appendage returned," Eliana joked, eagerly taking the replacement phone.

"Beckham filled us in. Any problems getting here?" Tiandra asked.

"No." Riker said. "He's got tracking skills because I can't figure out how he seems to stay a step ahead of us all the time."

"The incident at Todd's house was because we were in their territory," Eliana divulged then bit her lip.

Riker shook his head, annoyed.

"Sorry." She'd forgotten they weren't sharing that detail.

"You went to his house?" Skyler smacked his arm in a sisterly rebuke.

Riker rolled his eyes. "I needed information."

"And was that beneficial?" Tiandra prompted.

"No," Eliana replied. "Thanks to Ammo's warning, we escaped unharmed."

Skyler shot Riker a scolding glare.

"We learned Todd's in trouble with the Nites. If they figured out he murdered Moneyman and stole their money, he's on their kill list."

"And if they mistook you for Todd, they were probably watching his house for him to return," Tiandra agreed.

Skyler leaned against the wood railing. "We have information for you too. The results from CODIS arrived…" she began, referring to the FBI's Combined DNA Index System database. "And you won't believe what we found."

"Todd Billings recently lost his mother, Xenia, to cancer," Tiandra blurted over Skyler. At her teammate's vaulted look, Tiandra shrugged. "What?"

Skyler chuckled. "Go ahead."

"Before her death, Xenia sent DNA samples for herself and Todd to a popular genealogy website."

Tiandra's rapid-fire delivery had Eliana struggling to keep up.

"She was something else," Skyler interjected. "Neighbors called social services several times. At first, when witnesses saw Todd—just a little kid—wandering alone on the street at night. Later, they'd catch him dumpster-diving for food. The electricity was turned off multiple times."

"How sad," Eliana replied, a hand over her heart. Her father was a criminal, but he'd never left them so destitute. "No one should have to endure that."

"Agreed, but it doesn't give him the right to go after Riker," Tiandra said.

"And when we ran the DNA from the glove against the genealogy website sample, it was a match," Skyler said. "Todd's your identical twin."

Until that moment Riker had remained silent, but he replied, "But our birth dates are different."

Eliana's heart squeezed at the hurt and confusion in his voice.

"Only a week apart. We can explain that with delayed-interval delivery," Tiandra reminded them. "Once we get your adoption records, we'll confirm that finding."

"We're searching for Todd," Skyler assured him.

Riker shook his head. "Let's not jump to conclusions." He whistled for Ammo, snapping on his leash before he spun on his heel. "We need to go."

Eliana stood dumbfounded as Riker and Ammo walked away from her.

Tiandra touched her arm. "It's a lot to take in."

Skyler handed her an envelope. "Here's the information for your brother's case."

Eliana gaped. "How did you—"

Skyler smiled. "I have friends in Denver and since PHACE only requires the genetic variant report, they emailed it to me."

"If you find what you need there, we can request the physical sample to confirm the results," Tiandra added.

Touched by their kindness, Eliana clasped the envelope in both hands. "Thank you."

"You'd better hurry if you want to catch up with Riker. He's in his own world now and might forget you're with him," Skyler teased.

"Right." Eliana spun on her heel and jogged along the wooden platform until she reached Riker. True to Skyler's assessment, he appeared lost in his own thoughts.

The silence allowed Eliana to process her questions. How would they unravel this mess? What was Todd's motivation for trying to kill Riker?

By the time they reached the pickup, Eliana concluded one thing. Regardless of their understanding, it made sense to Todd.

Worse, would they find Todd before he found Riker?

Riker drove to his cabin on autopilot, unsure how he'd gotten there. Eliana had given him the space he'd needed to battle his thoughts. He sat quietly surveying the simple log structure set on the hilltop. Trees surrounded the property, and a partial decorative two-row log fence bordered the steps to the entrance.

Beckham and Graham stood waiting as they exited the truck. His commander agreed to continue patrolling the area, but Riker's distracted thoughts left him impatient. "We're safe here. You all did the recon and if you maintain perimeter surveillance, we'll be fine."

With only one dirt road leading to the cabin, it wasn't easily accessible from the highway.

"We'll be close." Beckham frowned. "See you at the next check-in time."

"Sure." Riker waved them off, eager to be alone with his thoughts.

His teammates drove off, leaving a dust whirling behind the vehicle.

The intensity of the news about Todd and Xenia Billings was more than he could bear, making him feel like he'd suffocate to death. But this place would provide the reprieve he needed and until he saw those adoption records, he refused to believe it all. Or at least to admit he believed it.

He released Ammo before collecting their bags. "Stay close, dude," he warned. His K-9 wagged his tail in compliance and trotted at his side as though he understood Riker's need for support.

Eliana joined him and moved to the log structure. She climbed the few steps and set the bags down while he unlocked the door.

She leaned over the porch railing. "The view is incredible here."

He moved toward her, relishing the familiar landscape that stretched beyond to the ravine and dipped down to the Niobrara River below. "Isaac and I built the wraparound porch because no matter where you stand, there's not a bad spot to enjoy the scenery."

"I can see why you like coming here."

He nodded and bowed his head. "I apologize for my quick retreat."

"No apology needed." She turned to face him. "You've got more than enough on your plate to deal with." The tender understanding in her expression brought a measure of comfort as her auburn tresses captured the sunlight.

Everything within him longed to pull her close and confess his fears of going to prison for a murder he hadn't committed. Along with the explosion of emotions at finding out he had a brother he'd never known existed, who wanted him dead for unknown reasons. After her vulnerable confession about Hunter and her father, how could he put those things on her? None of his problems was hers to bear.

"Yeah, there was never a class in the academy on how to deal with your murderous twin," he replied, sarcasm thick. He took a step back, distancing himself physically and emotionally.

A hint of sadness flickered in the gold around her emerald eyes. "Your team will find him."

The question remained when. Before Todd killed him? Before the mayor demanded Omaha PD charge him with murder. Finding Todd was the tip of the destruction iceberg in his life.

He nodded, unwilling to speak his concerns. Even if they found Todd, how would they prove he'd killed Moneyman?

Ammo strode along the porch, actively sniffing the bags and reminding Riker they should go inside.

He unlocked the door and pushed it wide.

This was where he needed to be. They'd be safe from Todd, or whoever was out to kill them, and get the information about his adoption.

"Not what I pictured," Eliana said, coming in behind him.

He blinked. "No? Why?"

"When you first mentioned a cabin, and I saw the gorgeous wraparound porch, I assumed the interior would be elaborate. This is…"

"Rustic?"

"Yes, that's the word," she replied.

He chuckled, glancing at the worn couch in front of the wood-burning stove.

She grinned. "No, it's nice. Really."

"You're a terrible liar."

That earned him a laugh. "I was trying to be polite."

"We have indoor plumbing, if that helps any."

"Oh, well then, I'm on board." She winked and walked outside.

Riker followed her, and they unloaded the rest of their belongings.

She moseyed around the dining table into the sparse kitchen and opened a cabinet. "This is an unexpected treat." She gestured to the well-stocked shelves and grocery bags on the short counter.

Emotion clogged Riker's throat. The team had thought of everything, even stacking logs beside the woodstove and, if he wasn't mistaken, they'd tidied up.

Except for the new porch, the cabin exterior appeared plain and unimpressive, which was how Riker had intended it to be. He ran his hand along the table. How could he explain to Eliana the importance of leaving everything as Grandpa had? There were hundreds of renovations he could make, but, somehow, maintaining the cabin the way his grandfather had, kept him alive here.

Ammo lumbered over to his lifted cot and settled onto it with a contented sigh.

"Sorry for blurting out about Todd's place," Eliana said, gaining his attention. He turned and walked to the kitchen where she sorted through the groceries.

Riker reached for a jar of spaghetti sauce and box of angel-hair pasta. Holding them up, he asked, "For dinner?"

"Sounds good."

"I deserved Skyler's scolding. I placed you in danger and I had no right to do that."

"It was my idea, remember? It's not like I went kicking and screaming," she quipped.

Together they unpacked the remaining groceries, placing them in the refrigerator and cabinets.

"They bought enough food to feed us for months. Makes me wonder if we're ever leaving."

Riker heard fear behind her teasing tone.

"It was nice of them to take care of us," Eliana said.

"They're the best." Riker's own sadness returned at the thought of being away from his team and unable to work the investigation. "I'll show you to your room." Hefting her bag, he led her to the only bedroom at the far side of the cabin. "The mattress is brand-new. Bathroom is right across the hall."

She surveyed the space. "Where will you sleep?"

"On the couch. It's a sleeper sofa." Though the coils would wreak havoc on his back. "Graham and Tiandra will return later for perimeter duty."

She entered the room and he set her bag beside the door. "I'd love to get that sample Skyler provided from my brother's case into PHACE."

"I'll leave you to work." Riker turned and walked to the living area, settling on the sofa. "Five minutes," he mumbled, closing his eyes.

A cold tongue swiped across his face. "Ammo," he groaned, forcing himself awake. His furry companion hovered close, panting. "There has to be a better way to wake me." Riker ruffled the dog's fur, catching a glimpse of his watch. He jerked upright. He'd slept for over five hours. Was Eliana okay? Jumping to his feet, he hurried to the bedroom, where she lay curled on her side, asleep, her laptop open beside her.

Riker exhaled relief and quietly exited the room, Ammo at his side. They headed outside and his K-9 trotted down the steps to the lawn. "Stick close, dude," he called, leaning over the rail to absorb the beautiful scenery.

Footsteps drew his attention and he turned.

"How long was I asleep?" Eliana smiled, and covered her mouth, hiding a yawn with one hand, the other holding her laptop.

Riker lifted his hands. "Dunno. I just woke up a few minutes ago too."

"We were both worn out." She moved beside him. "Please tell me you're not going hunting for our dinner?" she teased.

He laughed. "No. I hunt fugitives, not animals."

"Good. I want to show you something." She dropped onto the porch steps and opened the laptop.

"You've got my full attention." He sat beside her.

She removed her cell phone from her back pocket and set it in her lap. "Even though we don't have reception here, it's comforting to have a real phone again."

He chuckled. "An electronic security blanket?"

"Something like that." She grinned, studying the computer screen. "Aw. I thought it was done."

"What?"

"PHACE is still running the sample Skyler provided from my brother's case."

"Almost finished?"

"Yeah, about eighty-five percent. Once we have the composite, can we access the Denver DMV database?" she asked.

"When the team arrives tonight for the check-in, we'll send it with them," Riker said.

"Thanks. I'll be right back." She got to her feet and slid the phone into her back pocket. She hurried inside and returned without the laptop, then sat beside him again. "How will they search for Todd?"

Riker sighed, considering the question and unsure how to answer. "Identifying him was a huge part of the battle. He's bound to leave an electronic footprint."

"A beneficial aspect of technology," she teased.

"Touché." Riker smiled. "He can't hide forever, especially if he's made an enemy of the Nites. He needs my team to find him before they do."

"It's beautiful here."

Crickets chirped and the burbling of the river in the ravine below filled the peaceful atmosphere. The setting sun cast astounding splashes of orange, purple and blue across the sky. Ammo continued to wander the yard, nose to the ground, then made his way to them.

"Stick close, dude," Riker warned again, stroking the animal's brindle fur.

With a snort, Ammo returned to his perusal of the property, in full view.

"Guess he didn't like that idea." Eliana chuckled.

"He loves it out here, so he wants to wander."

"I don't blame him." She leaned back. "Before I lose my courage, I have a confession."

Riker fixed his gaze on her. "Okay."

"I should've told you about Hunter instead of hiding my motives for your team endorsing PHACE." Hanging her head, she said, "I'm ashamed of my selfishness and manipulation."

Riker moved in front of her, kneeling, and reached for her hands, enveloping them in his own. "I've read God gives us relationships in seasons. We met for a reason all those years ago and I'm honored you came to me for help."

She tilted her head and grinned. "At least you are now."

"Right." He waggled his eyebrows. "But it brought you back to me, and I'm grateful for that." Her hands were soft, and the scent of lavender wafted to him.

She squinted. "What're you saying?"

Riker refused to avert his eyes. He'd waited a long time for this moment. "My turn to confess before I lose my courage."

"Just say it fast," she encouraged.

"Eliana, our brief relationship in high school affected me more than I've ever admitted to anyone. Truth is, I fell head over heels for you." He tucked a stray lock of her hair behind her ear, grazing her cheek. "I knew the first day we met that you were the one. Do you believe in second chances?"

She blinked, absorbing him in her emerald irises. "Yes, I do. Isn't that God's specialty?"

"Definitely." He smiled.

"I needed a pruning and time to grow up," she sighed. "Guess I'm still trying to rid myself of baggage."

"Like?"

"Insecurity mostly." She shrugged but kept hold of his hands. "I wanted to be someone else. Someone prettier, smarter, basically anyone not me."

"You're a perfect version of you." Riker leaned closer, gaze lingering on her lips.

She met him in a tender kiss, tentative with apprehension. Riker reached up, interlacing his fingers in her hair, and gently deepened the kiss. The years of hurt melted in her sweet touch.

The moment ended too soon and he reluctantly released his hold. A soft blush covered her cheeks.

"Guess we'd better get dinner made," Eliana whispered.

Loath to move, he swallowed. "Yeah, any more of that might be dangerous." He smirked and she chuckled. "Ammo's probably starved by now."

A sharp bark startled Riker, and he jumped up, catching a blur of dark fur bolting into the heavy tree line and down the ravine.

"No!" Riker took off in a sprint, Eliana right behind him.

He helped her down the steep, narrow path to the river's edge, both shouting for Ammo.

Riker grabbed Eliana's hand. "We have to find him before it gets dark."

Thick tree cover and the last glimpses of light from the setting sun thrust them into twilight, making the search harder.

"Where is he?" Riker's heart hurt and worry consumed him. They couldn't stay outdoors for much longer. "Ammo!"

"Maybe he went home?" Eliana offered.

"I hope so." Riker shifted, leading the way back to the cabin. "We need to get inside." The words hurt to speak but he couldn't endanger Eliana any longer. "The next check-in is coming up. With all of us working, we'll find Ammo."

They climbed the ravine, alternating their calls for the dog. Riker held Eliana's hand, helping her to traverse the uneven ground.

When they reached the porch steps, Eliana entered the

darkened cabin ahead of him. As soon as Riker crossed the threshold, a force shoved him forward and the door slammed shut behind him. "Eliana!"

Light consumed the space and Riker blinked against the brightness, processing the mirror image holding Eliana hostage.

"Hello, big brother."

"Todd."

THIRTEEN

Eliana's hands grasped at Todd's hold around her throat. He'd moved lightning-fast, tugging her out of Riker's reach and covering her mouth before she could warn him. He'd kicked the door closed, trapping them.

"Let her go," Riker said, his hand slowly moving toward his gun.

Todd gave a sardonic laugh. "Reach for your weapon, and I'll snap her neck."

The oven-stove combination was to her right, and they backed up until they stood against the shortened kitchen counter.

Riker worked his jaw, his eyes narrow with a murderous glare. "She has nothing to do with this. I'm the one you're after."

"Spare me the heroic de-escalation junk. Put your gun on the floor and kick it to me." Todd pressed something hard against her temple and she winced. "Try anything cute, and I'll shoot a bullet into her brain before you fire the first round. Got it?"

"Yes." Riker lifted a hand in surrender. "I'm reaching for my gun." His compliance came painstakingly slow and Eliana wondered if he would shoot Todd.

"Hurry!" Todd tightened his hold around her neck.

Riker set his gun on the floor and kicked it to Todd.

The metal skidded across the wood, but Eliana couldn't see where it stopped.

"Now, sit in that chair," Todd ordered, his voice so much like Riker's.

Eyes on her, Riker complied. "What do you want?"

"That's a big question," Todd said. "We have lots to talk about before you die." He spoke against Eliana's ear, and she cringed at his closeness. "Make yourself useful and bind your boyfriend. Do it right, and don't try anything stupid, or I'll kill him. Understand?"

She nodded the best she could under his hold.

Then Todd addressed Riker. "If you even breathe wrong, I'll shoot her."

"You've made that clear," Riker growled.

Todd released and shoved Eliana forward. She gasped, filling her lungs with air as she stumbled into the dining table, spotting a set of black zip ties atop the wood. "Use those to secure his wrists and ankles to the spindles."

Eliana collected the zip ties and crossed the room to where Riker sat. Without a word, she did as Todd ordered, starting with Riker's wrists, then moving around and kneeling in front of him to finish the ankle bindings. Her eyes met Riker's, and she mouthed, *I'm sorry.* He worked his jaw and gave an almost imperceptible shake of his head.

"Quit making faces at each other," Todd barked. "Get back here!"

Eliana pushed to her feet and turned, facing Todd. For the first time since he'd taken them hostage, she saw his face. Unable to break her gaze, she stared in amazement at the remarkable resemblance to Riker. Only their clothing differed. Todd was dressed in a dark T-shirt displaying an image of an enlarged skull and crossbones, a denim jacket and black jeans. He'd even colored and styled his hair to match Riker's and included the facial hair stubble.

"Move!" Todd bellowed.

Eliana startled and scurried to where he stood.

"Don't try any tricks." He shoved her down hard on the chair in front of him. "You have no idea what I've already set into place. There might be a bomb, an incendiary device, who knows? I've more than proven my advanced skills."

Finding her voice, Eliana said, "You changed your appearance, Blaze."

"Aren't you observant?" His sardonic laugh boomed in the confined space. "I wanted my reunion with my big brother to be extra special." He slid behind her, encircling her wrists with what she assumed were similar zip ties, then repeated the action with her ankles.

"Let Eliana go. She's got nothing to do with this," Riker said again.

"Thanks to her interfering DNA phenotyping program, she's got everything to do with this," Todd argued.

"Where's my dog?" Riker snarled.

Todd shook his head. "That stupid mutt really was a pain in my plans. I had to take care of him." He moved behind Eliana. "I hoped he'd believe I was you, but turns out dogs are smarter than people."

"Did you hurt him?" Eliana gasped.

"I'm not a monster." He shifted into her line of sight. "Just tranquilized him."

Relief showed in Riker's expression, morphing into recognition. "That's my gun."

"Isn't that the best part?" Todd chuckled. "When the cops find your bodies in a sad murder-suicide act of desperation, your own weapon will testify against you."

"So why not shoot me, instead of this little tirade?" Riker pressed. "You have me here. What do you want?"

Todd paced behind her, cowardly using Eliana as a human shield. "You're so smart, brother, you tell me."

"You killed Moneyman and stole whatever cash he had

on him. Then you tried to pin it on me so you could disappear without the Nites hunting for you."

"Very good. See how simple the plan was?" Todd tsked. "But then you dragged her in." He pointed at Eliana with the gun, and she flinched. "And messed up everything."

"But why frame me? I never knew you existed before all this," Riker insisted. "What did I do to deserve this?"

Todd spun on his heel and stormed at Riker, fury engraved in his expression. "What did you do?" Without warning, he reared back and drove his fist into Riker's face with such force the chair rocked backward before righting on all four legs.

"No!" Eliana cried, jolting her own chair and teetering into the oven/stove.

Blood streamed from Riker's nose, but he remained stoic, pinning Todd with a venomous glare.

Todd stumbled as though he'd surprised himself with the action. "You ruined my life!"

Eliana's heart ached at the sight of Riker, defenseless against a man who hated him without cause. As if hearing her thoughts, Riker met her gaze and in that moment she saw the truth.

She loved Riker.

She'd always loved him, which was why she'd kept tabs on his progress. He'd never been far from her thoughts, and in her own cowardice, she'd waited for a good nonrelationship reason to contact him. *Liar.*

No, she'd waited to show him that she was more than a con man's daughter. She'd used PHACE to prove her worthiness.

Like a blinking billboard flashing her heart's truth, Eliana concluded that if Riker never agreed to endorse PHACE, she didn't care. She loved him.

Her only regret was not telling him before Todd killed them.

Todd stepped between them, facing Riker and eliminating her view of him. She had to do something. Shifting so she would feel the phone in her back jeans' pocket with her fingertips, a plan emerged. She couldn't call for help—they had no reception—but she could make sure they cleared Riker's name.

Eliana wriggled her fingers, slowly sliding the device free into one hand. She gripped it tightly as though her life depended on it.

Beckham had purchased an identical model to her previous phone, so she was familiar with the features without seeing the screen. It took a little finagling, but she pressed the side button to deactivate the sound. Then, using the oven's glass reflection, she activated her voice recording application while Todd continued raging at Riker.

She might not save them, but she'd ensure the police found the truth. She gently slid the phone into her pocket again and, using only her fingers, tugged her windbreaker down to cover the device. Like most killers she'd read about, Todd's ego and eagerness to impress them with his brilliant plan ensured she got his confession. Whatever it took, Eliana would make sure Riker's name was cleared. One last act of love.

"I'm sorry for your mother's recent passing," Eliana declared, hoping to prod Todd into communicating.

Todd spun to face her, wearing a strange expression, as though conflicted emotions warred within him. Eliana flinched. His finger hovered too close to the trigger. With his non-gun wielding hand, he reached up and touched the upper pocket on his denim jacket.

Eliana glanced over at Riker. What was Todd doing?

After several silent seconds, Todd said, "Can you love and hate someone at the same time?"

"Yes," Eliana said softly. "I experienced the same thing with my father."

Todd tilted his head as though studying her. A flash in

his eyes and the hardness returned to his face. "My worthless, spoiled brat of a twin was living the high life and I suffered!"

"I had no more choice over my parents than you did," Riker said.

Todd leaned against the stove. "You were just a victim of circumstance?" He scowled, revealing crooked tobacco-yellowed teeth. "Me too. I lived with a drug-addicted, abusive hag in that pit of a house."

"Todd, I never knew," Riker told him.

"Aw, would you have rescued me, big brother? Just like your perfect parents—smart move relocating them, by the way. Mother threw you away because you were defective. Your perfect parents didn't tell you that, did they?"

"Was Riker born first? Did they do delayed-interval delivery?" Eliana asked.

Todd glared at her. "How would I know?" He glanced at the gun in his hand.

"So why suddenly come after me?" Riker asked through his already-swelling split lip.

"Because while I was tending our dying mother, she asked me to give you a letter, then told me what a mistake she'd made by keeping me. But I did everything for her!"

Eliana gasped, gaining Todd's attention. "What's wrong, princess?" He knelt in front of her. "Was that a little harsh for you? Do you pity me?" He lifted a hand and Eliana flinched, berating herself for the weakness.

He laughed. "Oh, did your daddy beat you too?"

She frowned, and he pulled up his sleeve, revealing several circular marks. "Those are cigarette burns from one of my mother's many *admirers*."

"Leave her alone. It's not her fault your life was hard," Riker said.

Eliana shot him a thankful glance, but she refused to let him take the punishment for her. They needed to buy time. The next check-in had to be soon. If they kept Todd talking, maybe help would arrive in time. Either way, she was in no hurry to die.

"Your mother found Riker through the DNA genealogy website," Eliana persisted.

Todd tapped the side of his head with the tip of the gun. "See, that's why you're here. All you had to do was mind your own business. Then I saw your program on the news, and you had to die before you made the connection between Riker and me."

Eliana gasped. "You watched me?"

Todd's maniacal chuckle sent shivers down her back. "Of course, I did. Every chance I got. And there were many."

"But why frame Riker then try to kill him?" Eliana asked. "That made no sense."

"Moneyman had a big payout and I made sure everything pointed to you as his murderer. It was the perfect opportunity to reinvent myself by framing you." He jabbed a finger at Riker's chest. "I figured the Nites would handle the rest and kill you." He shook his head. "They're a bunch of idiots. They still came after me! I can't wait anymore. I need to get out of town. So, we'll finish up here with a nice murder-suicide to close the case once and for all. For everybody. The Nites included. That's why I didn't let you out of my sight. The Nites and your stupid team won't let this go until I tie up all the loose ends. Then I'll be on my way."

"No, you messed up. Something went wrong at the crime scene," Riker said.

Todd scowled. "The plan was perfect until your stupid dog interfered."

"Ammo?" Eliana didn't mask her confusion. "What did he have to do with anything?"

"He found the glove I lost."

Eliana blinked. "Wait, you didn't plant that for us to find?"

"He's not that smart," Riker countered.

In one stride, Todd lunged for Riker, planting another punch before pressing the gun against Riker's temple. "Smart enough to keep following you. Who's the smarter brother now?"

Riker shifted his gaze, fixated on Eliana. They locked eyes and his heart swelled, filling his chest with such intensity he thought he'd explode. He'd never stopped loving her. Why had he treated her return with such disdain when all he'd wanted was the chance to love her again? He should've told her sooner, but until this moment, he hadn't realized how much he needed her.

And now it was too late.

His career had taught him to fight for others, and he'd accepted death as a possible risk. All cops did. But something shifted. It wasn't just about winning the fight. Today, Riker would willingly lay down his life for Eliana's. All that mattered was that she survived. Whatever it took, he'd make that happen. *Lord, help me.*

"Let her go." Riker's voice was husky, tense with desperation.

"My program is in the bedroom. Destroy the computer and there's nothing for me to testify to. You escape, and no one has to die," Eliana pleaded.

Todd faced her, curiosity in his expression. "You know, I might just do that. After you're dead."

"There's still time to choose another way." Riker tried for reason. "What you seem to forget is our mother abandoned me. Not you. She chose you." He swallowed the painful words. Though a ruse, they hurt to speak aloud. "She threw me away because I was sick. If I'd known you existed, I would have found you. You're my brother."

Todd's expression softened slightly. He reached into his

jacket pocket and withdrew a folded piece of paper, studying it. "Too late. Besides, you already have one."

Riker's thoughts flew to Isaac, whom he hadn't seen since Christmas. He vowed if he lived, he'd make sure and change that immediately. But for now, he needed to reason with Todd. *Forgive me, Lord.* "Yeah, but it's different, not like us. We're blood-related."

Todd looked at the paper in his hand. "I used to wish for a sibling."

"You have that with Riker," Eliana inserted. "I'll destroy my computer. If you're worried I'll tell anyone, kill me. But let Riker go. Start over now and build a relationship with your brother."

Eliana's willingness to sacrifice herself for him had Riker doing a double take.

Todd glanced down, flipping the folded paper between his fingers. "I need a minute to think. I don't want to blow it now." He paced a path in front of them then moved toward the sofa.

She met Riker's eyes, and he mouthed, *Quiet*, while slowly freeing one hand. She nodded understanding.

Grateful she'd kept that binding looser than the other, he worked on tugging against the wooden spindle to free his other hand.

A slight rustle outside caught his attention, and he glanced at the open window beside the dining table. A breeze fluttered the curtains. Had he imagined the sound?

If he was wrong, they might be dead, but it would give him the diversion he needed. Another rustle. *"Aanval!"* Riker hollered the Dutch command for attack.

Todd spun around, gun positioned at Riker, and fired.

Dark fur blurred in Riker's peripheral vision as he scurried back, ankles still bound, and slammed against the door. The wooden chair splintered apart, freeing him.

Ammo barreled through the screen, skidding across the

dining table, and landed on the floor, teeth bared. He lunged and clamped down on Todd's gun-wielding arm. Another shot exploded before Todd dropped the gun.

He howled in pain, and Ammo remained engaged.

"Vrijlaten!" Riker hollered the command for release.

"Call him off!" Todd pleaded.

"Vrijlaten!" Riker repeated.

The K-9 released his hold and backed in a stalking stance to Riker's side. Todd lunged over the coffee table, running for the door. Ammo tackled him from behind, and Todd slammed face-first to the floor. Splayed with his hands outstretched, he whimpered, "Okay, okay."

Ammo stood beside him, growling, teeth bared.

Riker snagged the gun and turned toward Eliana.

Tiandra and Graham bolted through the front door, hollering orders of "Get down!" and "Hands behind your head!"

"Ammo. Here." Riker moved to Eliana and freed her from the bindings. He pulled her into his arms as Ammo trotted to his side. "Are you okay?"

"I am now." She melted into his embrace.

Ammo barked, and they knelt, praising the dog with a thorough rub. "Great job, dude!"

Todd hollered, "It's not fair!" as Graham hauled him, handcuffed, out of the cabin.

Tiandra followed behind. "I'll be right back."

The paper Todd had flung on the table fluttered with the breeze. Riker unfolded the worn document and read it aloud for Eliana.

"'Dear Riker. If this letter finds you, I'm probably dead. Never should've waited so long to look for you. My biggest regret was giving you up instead of Todd. You needed better than I could give anyway. You always were better than us. Even as a baby. I love you. Always have. Thought of you often too. Hope you thought of me. Mother.'"

Compassion swelled in Eliana's eyes. "Wow." She pulled him into a side hug.

"Todd endured abuse and neglect while I lived with the most amazing parents in the world. He's right. How unfair is that?" Riker asked.

"But that's not your fault," Eliana said. "Todd's anger and resentment is his own to bear. He didn't have to turn out that way."

"I feel sorry for him," Riker admitted. "If my parents hadn't raised me to love God and forgive others, I could've ended up like Todd."

"No arguments there," Eliana said. She stared at him then pulled back. "You should be seen by a doctor. He punched you pretty hard."

"I'm fine."

"At least let me help you clean up." She quickly retrieved a damp cloth from the kitchen and gently washed the blood from his face, her movements slow and tender.

After she was finished, they walked out to the porch where Todd sat in the back seat of Graham's car.

"I need to talk to him," Riker said.

Graham opened the door but stood guard.

Riker approached and exhaled. *God, please give me the words to speak.* "Todd, you've put yourself in a dangerous position with the Nites. Cooperate with us and provide the big players so we can take them down."

"No way."

"Once they learn the truth of what you've done, you'll be on their kill list."

"I'll take my chances," Todd snorted. "You've got nothing to charge me with Moneyman's death. Plus, Noella will protect me."

Riker gawked. "She was working with you to make it look like you were really me?"

"Money buys allegiance," Todd replied coolly.

"What about Officer Marvin?" Riker asked.

"Never heard of him," Todd replied.

"Actually." Eliana moved between them and withdrew her cell phone. "We have your recorded confession."

"You did what?" Riker spun to face her. "How?"

She lifted a shoulder. "If we didn't get out of the situation alive, I wanted to make sure your name was cleared. You deserve for the world to know that you're a great man, Riker Kastell."

Riker's throat constricted, emotions rising within him. "You're an amazing lady, Eliana. Thank you."

Todd's mouth gaped with the revelation.

Pity for his brother overrode his anger. "Todd, take the deal. Your life literally depends on it."

"Who cares if I die?" Todd looked down, defeat written all over him.

"I do," Riker said. "If you'll agree to seek help, maybe we could get to know each other."

His twin's head snapped up. "Why would I want that?"

Riker shrugged. "Because you realize it's a better use of your time. Your life is up to you. Whatever you choose, I forgive you."

"I don't need your forgiveness," Todd snapped.

"You'll have plenty of time to think about it," Graham said.

"Hey, get this," Tiandra said, joining them. "Joy ran the hair from Riker's crime scene."

"But I thought it didn't have the root?" Riker asked.

"She had just enough to test it against Xenia's genealogy sample," Tiandra explained.

"It's a match for you, Todd," Graham said.

Todd swallowed hard, his rebellious attitude deflating.

"Now's a good time to give up any information to save yourself. The Nites will find out you betrayed them," Riker warned.

Todd hung his head. "Fine. I'll tell you whatever you want. If you protect me."

"We'll make sure you're alive to stand trial," Tiandra assured him, closing the passenger door. "Graham and I will take care of booking him and protective detail."

"Thank you," Riker said.

Graham slid in behind the wheel and closed the door.

Tiandra put a hand on her hip, sporting a mischievous grin. "I'm glad to see you two finally figured out your feelings for one another."

"You knew?" Eliana asked.

"We're trained observers." Tiandra winked and playfully punched Riker in the shoulder.

"Oh, wait! Hold on!" Eliana ran into the cabin.

Tiandra and Riker exchanged glances.

Graham rolled down the window. "What's wrong?"

"Eliana has something," Tiandra said.

She returned, carrying her open laptop. "Here's the PHACE composite from the sample taken at my brother's murder scene. Would you run it in against the DMV database for an identity?"

Riker studied it. "No need."

"Nope, that's Javier Zinga," Tiandra said.

"He's a known Nite," Graham noted.

"So, you'll arrest him?" Eliana asked, excitement in her voice.

Riker reached for her, pulling her closer. "He died in prison two years ago."

Eliana exhaled and closed the laptop. "Then I guess it's over."

"Yes, but I'm sorry we can't charge Zinga formally," Riker said.

"At least Hunter's case is closed." She sighed. "Thank you all for your help."

"I'm sorry for your loss," Tiandra replied, touching Eliana's arm. "On the bright side, you'll have our team's endorsement for PHACE. What do you think, Riker?"

"Absolutely."

"You've got my vote," Graham said.

Eliana glanced up, eyes shimmering. "After I add the multiple-birth caveat into the program."

Ammo sidled up beside Riker. "Looks like he's ready to come out of retirement," Graham added.

Riker nodded, stroking the dog's fur. "His hearing seems to be improving."

"We'd better get going," Graham said, and Tiandra rounded the vehicle, climbing into the passenger seat. "But we'll be back. Can't leave you two alone," he winked.

"We'll have dinner ready," Riker replied, chuckling.

As the taillights faded from sight, Eliana held the laptop against her chest. "Todd needs a lot of prayer and therapy."

"I hope he gets both," Riker said. "I plan to do what I can to help him."

"If you'll let me, I'd like to be there to support you when you do."

He blinked and turned, embracing her. "Eliana, the one thing I realized in all of this is that I love you. I always have. If you're willing, I want to take a lifetime to show you just how much."

She rose on her toes to meet his lips and kissed him. "The entire time Todd held us hostage, all I could think about, besides escaping, was how I'd never told you I love you."

Riker blinked. "You do?"

"Yes."

He held her tighter. "With Todd identifying the Nites, my parents will be home in no time."

"What a perfect way to start our lives together."

Riker swiped at his forehead. "That was a serious workout. I'm ready for dinner."

"Me too."

They returned to the cabin, and Ammo climbed onto his cot, stretching out. "He's tired too." Riker smiled, preparing their spaghetti dinner. "I can't believe you were willing to sacrifice PHACE to save me."

"I'd do anything for you," Eliana said.

Abandoning the meal, he pulled her close again. "How about a fall wedding?"

EPILOGUE

Two months later...

Riker and Eliana entered the task force headquarters where the team and dogs had already assembled. Ammo trotted beside them, and they took their places around the conference table. "So, we've got an update?" Riker asked.

"That's what Beckham said," Graham replied.

Eliana removed her laptop from her bag and began logging into her program. They'd worked endlessly to bring down the last of the big D'Alfo Nites's players. With all but one leader in custody, the lower-level gang members had scattered.

Beckham strode from his office into the Rock, his mood solemn as he dropped to the seat across from Eliana.

The team exchanged worried glances. Was there bad news?

Though his job had consumed his every waking hour for years, reuniting with Eliana had adjusted Riker's priorities. No matter what came, with her by his side, he felt invincible. As if sensing his adoration, she glanced at him and smiled. He enveloped her right hand in his. Could he fall any deeper in love with this woman?

"You two are adorable," Skyler said.

Riker chuckled. "I'm okay with never being told I'm 'adorable,' just so you know."

Eliana leaned back and laughed.

"It's good to have everyone together again…" Beckham began, calling the meeting to order.

Cries of *hear, hears* and *amens* filled the space.

Riker released her hand, allowing Eliana to resume working on her laptop. Her diamond engagement ring caught the overhead light, casting rainbow prisms around the room.

Tiandra shielded her eyes with one hand. "I need sunglasses if she's going to wear that in meetings," she teased.

"Sorry." Eliana blushed. "It's Riker's fault. He picked it out."

"I think Riker should've bought all of us one," Skyler quipped.

"I'd look good in one of those." Graham extended his hand as though admiring an imaginary ring on his finger.

Riker chuckled. "Eliana's the only one getting a ring."

"When's the big day?" Graham asked.

"Hopefully soon," Riker said, glancing at Beckham. "Since returning home and hearing the news of our engagement, my parents have committed to being our full-time wedding coordinators."

Eliana laughed. "Stop. They're wonderful and I love them."

His commander remained stoic.

The day couldn't come fast enough for Riker. Todd's arrest and confession had cleared him of all charges, and they'd arrested most of the Nites's key players. Riker grew antsy to make Eliana his wife and begin their lives together. They had too many dreams on hold.

"Let's focus, people." The room grew quiet as they waited for the commander to continue. Finally, Beckham said, "We got word just moments ago that Nebraska State Troopers arrested the last of the Nites's leaders Todd provided."

A collective cheer erupted.

"D'Alfo Nites are done!" Riker and Graham leaped to their feet and high-fived over the table.

Eliana stood. "That's great news!"

"Let Operation 'Wedding Planning' commence," Skyler commented.

"Quiet down, there's more," Beckham said. "I called you all here to share some information." The team returned to their professional demeanors as he passed manila folders to each member. "Eliana, has PHACE completed the sample I provided to you earlier?"

She nodded and typed on her laptop. "Just about." Scooting away from the table, she busied herself connecting her computer to the monitors. The screens came to life with the PHACE logo, ready for her to display the results.

"Who's our new fugitive?" Graham asked.

"This one falls into a different category," Beckham replied cryptically.

Riker had to bite his lip to keep from speaking.

Eliana returned to her seat. "It's loading," she announced.

The group continued their light bantering, but Riker's gaze remained fixed on the screen. When the facial composite finished, the conversation stilled.

Eliana gasped. "Um, sir. That's me."

"This is the face of our new computer technology director," Beckham said, grinning wide as a Cheshire cat.

Eliana blinked several times.

"It's official," Beckham continued. "Eliana Daines, soon to be Eliana Kastell, the Heartland Fugitive Task Force would like to extend the offer of a full-time, permanent position to join our team."

Eliana's eyes widened to the size of dinner plates, and she faced Riker. "Did you know about this?"

Riker was practically bursting inside, yet he remained

nonchalant and lifted his hands in surrender. "He needed a sample of your hair."

"Well, what do you think?" Skyler prodded.

"Yes! Yes!" Eliana exclaimed, jumping to her feet. "Thank you! I'm thrilled and honored to be a member of such an elite team."

"She didn't get that excited when I asked her to marry me," Riker teased.

She playfully swatted at him then leaned over, allowing him to kiss her.

"Hey, no PDA," Graham whined, referencing their public display of affection.

Eliana dropped back into her seat, beaming and blushing.

"We have more good news," Riker said. He allowed the momentary silence to increase the suspense.

"Riker, if you don't tell us…" Skyler warned with a grin.

He smiled and lifted a hand. "Patience, Skyler, patience."

She returned a playful glower.

"Riker, just spill it," Eliana probed.

"Ammo passed his auditory tests and is recertified," Riker announced. "He is officially out of retirement."

"Outstanding!" Beckham said, along with the rest of the team's applause.

"Welcome back, Ammo." Tiandra ruffled his fur.

The dog sat panting happily, a smile on his canine face, absorbing the attention.

Eliana reached below the table and produced the box of treats they'd brought for the K-9s. "We wanted to celebrate with you all."

Graham wrinkled his nose. "Did you bring treats for us too?"

"Why, of course I did." The baritone voice spun Riker like a top. Nelson stood in the doorway, holding a bakery box. "Mind if I join the party?"

"Nelson!" Shoving back his chair, Riker embraced his friend and led him to an open seat at the table.

Once they passed around plates with enormous slices of chocolate cake, Nelson said, "The only thing missing are fries."

Riker laughed, his heart overflowing with gratitude for the blessings in his life. "We'll have them served in platters at the wedding."

* * * * *

*If you enjoyed this story,
look for these other books
by Sharee Stover:*

Cold Case Trail
Tracking Concealed Evidence

Dear Reader,

Thank you for taking time to share Eliana and Riker's story with me. I hope you enjoyed their adventures. I love forensics, and when I first began my research into DNA phenotyping, story ideas abounded!

Not everyone is a fan of technology. Certainly not Riker. He has good cause to feel the way he does, considering the injustices he's seen. In contrast, Eliana finds technology to be important in solving her brother's cold case. Their personal experiences mold their outlook on technology, life and justice. One sees hope in the advances, the other sees disaster.

The battle of brother against brother is as old as Cain and Abel. The only thing that changes hate is the love of God. Our personal experience paints a huge portion of our view of life, good and bad. None of us escapes hurt, but with God, we can exchange our sorrow for joy. He's taken our mourning and turned it into dancing (Psalm 30:11) and we're adopted into God's family, accepted and loved (Ephesians 1:5). What wonderful news! We have the best Father!

I love hearing from you, so let's stay in touch. Join my newsletter, where you'll be the first to hear about my new releases and get behind the scenes of my books. Sign up or contact me at my website, www.shareestover.com.

Blessings to you,
Sharee

LISCNM1222

Get 4 FREE REWARDS!

We'll send you 2 FREE Books plus 2 FREE Mystery Gifts.

FREE
Value Over
$20

Both the **Love Inspired®** and **Love Inspired® Suspense** series feature compelling novels filled with inspirational romance, faith, forgiveness, and hope.

YES! Please send me 2 FREE novels from the Love Inspired or Love Inspired Suspense series and my 2 FREE gifts (gifts are worth about $10 retail). After receiving them, if I don't wish to receive any more books, I can return the shipping statement marked "cancel." If I don't cancel, I will receive 6 brand-new Love Inspired Larger-Print books or Love Inspired Suspense Larger-Print books every month and be billed just $6.24 each in the U.S. or $6.49 each in Canada. That is a savings of at least 17% off the cover price. It's quite a bargain! Shipping and handling is just 50¢ per book in the U.S. and $1.25 per book in Canada.* I understand that accepting the 2 free books and gifts places me under no obligation to buy anything. I can always return a shipment and cancel at any time by calling the number below. The free books and gifts are mine to keep no matter what I decide.

Choose one: ☐ **Love Inspired**
Larger-Print
(122/322 IDN GRDF)

☐ **Love Inspired Suspense**
Larger-Print
(107/307 IDN GRDF)

Name (please print)

Address   Apt. #

City   State/Province   Zip/Postal Code

Email: Please check this box ☐ if you would like to receive newsletters and promotional emails from Harlequin Enterprises ULC and its affiliates. You can unsubscribe anytime.

Mail to the Harlequin Reader Service:
IN U.S.A.: P.O. Box 1341, Buffalo, NY 14240-8531
IN CANADA: P.O. Box 603, Fort Erie, Ontario L2A 5X3

Want to try 2 free books from another series? Call **1-800-873-8635** or visit www.ReaderService.com.

LIRLIS22R2

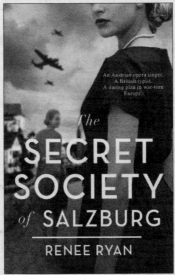